SECOND CHANCES

harriet zaidman

Red Deer Press

SECOND CHANCES

harriet zaidman

Published in Canada by Red Deer Press,
195 Allstate Parkway, Markham, ON L3R 4T8

Published in the United States by Red Deer Press,
311 Washington Street, Brighton, MA 02135

Red Deer Press acknowledges with thanks the Canada Council for the Arts
and the Ontario Arts Council for their support of our publishing program.
We acknowledge the financial support of the Government of Canada through the
Canada Book Fund (CBF) for our publishing activities.

Edited for the Press by Peter Carver
Text and cover design by Tanya Montini
Proudly printed in Canada by Avant Imaging & Integrated Media

Library and Archives Canada Cataloguing in Publication

Title: Second chances / Harriet Zaidman.
Names: Zaidman, Harriet, 1952- author.
Identifiers: Canadiana 20210209607 | ISBN 9780889956391 (softcover)
Subjects: LCGFT: Novels.
Classification: LCC PS8649.A382 S43 2021 | DDC jC813/.6—dc23

Publisher Cataloging-in-Publication Data (U.S.)

Names: Zaidman, Harriet, 1952-, author.
Title: Second Chances / Harriet Zaidman.
Description: Markham, Ontario : Red Deer Press, 2021.| Summary: "Dale Melnyk, who plays
goal for his community hockey team and dreams of playing in the NHL someday, suddenly finds
himself gasping in an iron lung. Like other young polio victims in Winnipeg in 1955, Dale's life is
upended. As he fights back, he learns some hard realities about the disease – and also about the
racism lurking in the city" -- Provided by publisher.
Identifiers: ISBN 978-0-88995-639-1 (paperback)
Subjects: LCSH Hockey players -- Juvenile fiction. | Poliomyelitis – Patients -- Juvenile fiction. |
Racism – Juvenile fiction. | BISAC: YOUNG ADULT FICTION / General.
Classification: LCC PZ7.Z353Se |DDC 813.6 – dc23

Red Deer Press

www.reddeerpress.com

For Cecil, with love – H

CHAPTER ONE

In and out, in and out, the air moved at a steady beat. Summoning all his willpower, Dale gritted his jaw and tightened the muscles in his neck as best he could. A jab of pain shot through his throat. Squeezing his eyes shut, he felt warm tears trickling out the corners, edging slowly along his temples.

His willpower, though, was no match for the machine. Dale fought for control, but the pull on his chest was unrelenting. The machine drew life-giving oxygen through the tube, expanding his lungs. A moment later, the pressure was reversed, and he had to expel the carbon dioxide, the process repeating at an even, robot-like rate, the motor vibrating below. The machine didn't care whether he wanted to breathe or not. He was immobile, and he could only assume his arms and hands were lying flat at his side. He didn't know. His legs, which once propelled him forward at blinding speed, were now useless sticks he couldn't see.

He tried moving his head but got nowhere. A twinge shot through his neck, reminding him of the pipe sticking out below his Adam's apple. That's what he and his friends called it when they yodeled like mountaineers in the locker room, the bump on their throats jiggling up and down, the sound echoing off the walls, along with their laughter and banter. Here, though, the voices called it a larynx. He couldn't move it, and it hurt. And because he couldn't move his head, he had to look at his new self in the mirror above him. His head lay on a smooth aluminum tray, a folded towel for a pillow. His pale skin and flattened hair repelled him. The collar around his neck chafed his skin.

How long had he been like this? It seemed like only a day or two since he and Paul had been playing hockey on the street. At any other time, he would have recorded in his diary how new experiences made him feel, so he would remember them. Now, he wanted to forget everything.

He tried to interrupt the machine again, and again he failed. He swallowed hard, casting his thoughts about for another way to defeat it. He could feel the buildup of mucus in his throat. Maybe, he decided, he wouldn't cough. The tube would fill up, blocking the unwanted air from slipping in. Then he and his sorrow could drown together, silently. He decided to keep still and let it happen. He was hidden by the white cloth screen the voices had placed around his machine, but forgotten to remove when they'd last worked on him. Now was his chance. The screen would hide the twisted expression on his face; he hoped the noise of all the other machines in the room would conceal any sounds he made.

But his cough reflex kicked in and he choked loudly. From out of nowhere, the screen was whisked away. Two hands appeared above him, slipping a narrow hose into the tube in his throat, suctioning up the guck. The hands cleaned up the edges of the tube with a washcloth. Without making eye contact, the person behind the white mask used a hand to give Dale's hair a brief pat. "There," a woman's voice behind the mask pronounced. "All better now." The hands and the faceless being disappeared.

The air came back, fresher than before. High above him, the white ceiling was his sky. He tried to sigh, but the iron lung deprived him of even a moment's personal despair. In and out, in and out, evenly, unrelentingly. Again, the mirror reflected his unhappy face.

"Mom ..." He tried to call out, but his voice came out as a gurgle.

How could he die if everything and everyone was trying to keep him alive?

CHAPTER 2

"Here I come!"

Dale leaned forward and planted his boots firmly on the pavement, his eyes on the red, blue, and white rubber ball racing toward him. He gripped his goalie stick, shifting it between his knees as Paul deked from side to side, avoiding little patches of ice on the road. The ball slid and bounced ahead of the stick but couldn't escape Paul's blade. Dale's senses went on high alert, anticipating his friend's best efforts to get the ball past him.

A split second later, the whack came. The ball sailed high on the right. Dale pulled himself back up and shot his right arm out, snapping the ball from the air with his hand. The shock stung his palm through his thin gloves; in that moment, Dale wished he had the soft goalie mitt that could protect his hand against the blow of the puck. He'd had to turn the mitt in at the end of the hockey season.

But this was street hockey—no cushioned mitts, and a ball instead of a puck. The ball bounced back, harmless now, and headed straight for the water by the curb.

"Not in the puddle!" Paul wailed, as it disappeared into the murky mess. "Anyway, that was a good save, Dale."

"Good shot," Dale said.

Paul veered to the dry spot on the road and stuck his shoes into his rubber boots. "I loved puddles when I was little," he laughed and waded into the water. Using the blade of his hockey stick, he fished around until he found the ball, flipping it out onto the road.

Dale stretched his back and undid the buttons on his jacket. The late afternoon sun was warm enough to make him sweat, but the air had cooled enough to give him relief—the contradiction of April. He tapped his stick on one of the jam pails that served as goal posts. A car turned down Smithfield Avenue and slowed as it approached the boys. Dale picked up the pails on either side of him and held them until the car passed. More families had cars these days, and some fathers would be arriving home from work in the next half-hour. But he and Paul still had time to play without much disruption.

Usually, he liked to play street hockey after school,

especially since the Bantam B playoffs had ended a few weeks earlier. He'd had his best season ever as goalie, but it had been long and tough. He nursed a hope that his dream of being scouted for the NHL one day could be a reality, and his coach agreed it was possible. But his back and neck had been aching all afternoon, and all he really wanted to do was flop down on the couch at home.

Paul rolled the ball toward him at a leisurely pace.

"Do you think we can win the championship next year?" Dale mused, leaning on his stick to ease the nagging in his back. "It's the last year before we move up to Bantam A."

"We just missed it, didn't we?" Paul said, stick-handling the ball back and forth, while trying to scrape off the layer of grit it had accumulated. "Their offense was better than ours. Nothing you could have done about it. We only lost by one point."

"I hope those new kids coming up next year will make a difference. Mr. Leah said he's going to give them extra coaching time. At least we're solid," Dale said, tapping Paul's calf with the blade of his stick. "Dale Melnyk the Mighty, and Paul Alexander the Great—two of the best goalies in town."

Paul didn't reply. Dale decided his aches were in his head. "Let's go again. You're in net," he challenged. Paul twisted his mouth back and forth and headed for the net.

Dale picked up the ball, rubbed the rest of the dirt away with his glove, and dropped it to the pavement. Paul crouched down in the goal crease, his knees folded in like a butterfly's wings to stop the puck. Dale modeled his own stance after Terry Sawchuk, the winningest goalie for the Detroit Red Wings. Sawchuk flung his body in whatever direction the puck came flying, and whacked it down. Dale noticed that the picture Sawchuk used for hockey cards showed him as a younger man, before his teeth had been knocked out and his face marked by slap shots. Dale hoped his face would never accumulate the same number of scars as Sawchuk's had from the high velocity hits he'd taken.

But a goalie's face was another barrier to an opponent getting a point, so Dale assumed that might be his fate, too. He ran his tongue over his front teeth, proud of their smooth feel, and the way they looked bright and white when he smiled. He didn't like the thought of having a hole in his smile.

"Let's see if the backup can beat the star," Paul

taunted. Dale came back to attention, took in a breath, and began circling with the ball, hoping to put Paul off guard. He faked left and right, then turned around again.

"Chicken!" Paul laughed. "Come on, Melnyk."

Dale began his assault, shifting his hips, his rubber boots scraping as he skate-slided from side to side, his open jacket flapping. The roughness of the cement slowed the ball, but he managed to control its direction. He tipped his eyes to Paul's left, and, knowing his friend's one weakness, saw Paul move in to guard the left jam pail. Instantly, Dale switched and drove the ball toward the space on Paul's right side.

But Paul's right leg sliced through the air and stopped the ball, "Got it!" Paul yelled, popping up in the net. "Got it!" The ball bounced back limply at Dale.

"How did you do that?" Dale asked, more in surprise than for information. Misjudging fakes was Paul's weakness, the reason he was the backup rather than the starter.

"Practice makes better," Paul said, tapping his stick on the road. "Isn't that what Mr. Leah always says?"

"Yeah! He'll be impressed, for sure. That was a great save. You really will be Alexander the Great."

Paul laughed at the nickname. "My dad and I have been working on it."

"Hey, it shows," Dale said. "It's going to be a tight fight for the starter's spot next year." He couldn't believe he was saying this. Everything had always been the same between him and Paul. The two boys had been best friends since they met at Seven Oaks School in Grade 1. They discovered they lived only two blocks apart, and as they grew up, they visited each other's houses several times a week, so much that their mothers routinely cooked and baked extra food, because they assumed another serving would be required.

The city flooded neighborhood playgrounds each winter, and the boys learned to skate and scrimmage with hockey players of all ages who turned up on the ice nearly every day. Dale and Paul picked up a range of skills and tips from the older boys. When they were alone on the rink, they practiced hard, racing from one end to the other, both of them getting faster and stronger. All spring, summer, and fall, they'd kept their game up, too, using one of Paul's sister's bouncy rubber balls. They were a team by themselves. Their years of work paid off when they were old enough to join a community league. They made it through the tryouts, and jumped for joy when they saw both their names posted on the bulletin board outside the coach's office at the Perth Community Center. It was a great day for the two friends.

Now, Dale had to admit, because they both loved hockey so much, it caused tension between them. Both of them skated well and could score, but they both gravitated toward the goal crease, thrilled to test their reflexes and keep the rubber disk out of the net. Every year on every team, the different coaches chose them both as goalies, but every year on every team, they anointed Dale as the starter. Paul was good, but Dale was slightly better. Just slightly.

Cracks had begun to appear in their relationship—Dale realized they were becoming rivals. They never talked about it. They kept practicing, giving each other advice about the way they stood, analyzing each other's weaknesses, and trying out ways to correct them. They were feared by the best players on the opposing teams for their rapid responses. In the regular season, Paul got plenty of ice time, winning a lot of games for the team, helping to vault them into the playoffs. But Dale was the starter and filled the goalie job, as the team advanced into the championships. Now, Dale had to admit, there was tension between them, and it was because they both loved hockey so much.

Even when Dale's mother died, he still showed up to play hockey. Mr. Leah put him in net because it was best for the team. Dale never heard Paul question the coach's decision.

Dale thought Paul was okay with the way things were. They were also in the same Grade 8 class in school. Paul called on Dale every morning, and they talked about hockey while they walked together to Edmund Partridge Junior High. Then they practiced hockey after school and on weekends. Best friends.

"I have something to tell you," Paul said, his eyes down.

Dale leaned on his stick, glancing down at the pencil marks he'd inscribed on its shaft, a record of all his games. He wanted to go home and take it easy, maybe have a snack. He didn't know what was wrong, but his back and neck hurt, no matter how hard he tried to ignore the aches. He didn't want a long conversation.

"I might move," Paul said.

"Move?" Dale snapped his head back. His neck really hurt now. "Where? Why? You can't move! When?"

Paul waited a moment before answering. "Well, I wouldn't really move, but my dad says I should tell the hockey league I'm living with my grandma and grandpa on Boyd Avenue. That way I can play for Northwood Community Center. My dad knows the coach there, Mr. Lefteruk. I met him, too. He said he saw me at the tournament in February. The team has an opening for a goalie next year, and Mr. Lefteruk says I could make it."

"What?"

"I'll go back and forth between houses—my official address will be at my grandparents', though. I know it's cheating a bit, but that's the only way I can play for Northwood," Paul continued. "My mom and dad talked about it. My grandparents are sort of excited about the idea, too. But I'll still come back to my real home on the weekends." He clicked his tongue. "We can see each other then," he added, his eye catching Dale's briefly before he looked down again.

"But if you change your address, you have to change schools. That's the rule." Dale's head spun at this terrible news. First his mother had died, and now his best friend was leaving him and their team. "We won't be in the same school anymore, never mind the same class. That's crazy! Why do you want to do that?" A wave of nausea and panic roiled up inside of him.

"Yeah, I'll have to change schools," Paul said slowly, digging the blade of his stick into the cement. "But I want to get better at hockey, Dale, and the way to do that is to play more. I don't get to do that when you're in net most of the time." He paused. "Anyway, my dad's looking into the arrangements."

"And you're just telling me now? What about our team?" Dale's head throbbed, and he wasn't sure, but he thought he might be shouting. Another car approached. The boys each picked up a pail and moved to opposite sides of the street. The car passed between them.

Paul didn't seem to be as upset as Dale. He swung his pail. The rocks inside rattled. "I'm never going to start unless I go somewhere else," he said. "It's not your fault. You're good, that's all. I'll see you here on weekends and I'll see you at games—but on the opposite team." He swung his pail again, still keeping his eyes down.

Silence hung in the air. Paul shook the pail, the clanking stones breaking the silence. "Mr. Lefteruk likes my style, too. He thinks more goalies will use the butterfly style soon and he wants to help me with it." He squeezed out a weak smile. "Maybe I'm not good as a backup. I don't throw up before every game, like Glenn Hall does, and I do try to be like him." He pretended to smile again.

Dale didn't find the lame joke funny at all. Glenn Hall was a great backup goalie for Detroit, who used the new butterfly style, crouching in the crease and turning his knees with blistering speed to catch the puck, but everyone also knew he got sick to the stomach before every game, which he and Paul thought was weird. Dale knew Paul wanted more, but he never expected anything to really change.

Maybe Glenn Hall didn't like playing second fiddle to Terry Sawchuk, either. Maybe that's why he threw up before every game—he was upset, not nervous.

"What about the team? What about our chances? Did you tell Mr. Leah?" he asked.

"Uh ... not yet. I didn't. I will ... or my dad will— soon." Paul sighed and shrugged. "The team—well, I guess everyone leaves in the end, don't they? They'll have you, Dale, so their chances are still pretty good—

unless I beat you," he said quietly. He sighed again. "Anyway, I have to go home. I want to get my homework finished before the game." Then he added, "I don't think I'll be able to come over tonight, either."

Dale felt another blow. "What do you mean? It's the final game of the Stanley Cup series. We always listen to it together. Terry Sawchuk is going to be on his game tonight. This is important." He knew his voice was rising and he felt hotter.

"Uh ... my grandparents bought a television. We're going there to watch it," Paul replied. "I really like watching the action at the same time as it happens. It's even more exciting than radio. If I'm going to live there, I can watch it all the time. Think how much my game can improve if I can see what they do." He turned to Dale. "Are you getting one?"

"Doubt it," Dale said, now feeling as if his voice had disappeared. He was exhausted, and now he had to admit there was a problem in his family. "They're really expensive, and my dad is counting every penny now, even more than he used to. I saw one in a store window for $249. If I asked, he'd tell me to pay better attention to the play-by-play on the radio. He would probably spend his money on a car before anything else. He loves fixing them at the garage. I won't even ask." He felt embarrassed at what he'd said.

"Ah, that's tough. Maybe you can come over sometimes to my grandparents' place, or our house. My parents are talking about it, saving up, you know? Hey, you really think you can ever be as good as Sawchuk?" Paul asked, acting as if things were the same as ever, as if he hadn't delivered his blockbuster news. He pocketed the ball and picked up his schoolbooks from a dry spot on the curb. He slung his stick over his shoulder.

The pail was usually a featherweight in Dale's hands. He and Paul had each contributed containers that held their families' favorite jams—Dale liked to slather his toast with strawberry jam, while Paul's favorite was orange marmalade—then they washed away the sticky fruit and loaded the pails up with rocks they found in their backyard and along the back lanes. Today, he found his pail as heavy as if it were weighted with lead.

He'd been tired for a few days, he realized. The end of the hockey season had been so intense and exciting, and combined with doing schoolwork, he thought he still hadn't caught up on his sleep. Now he had to worry about losing his friend, as well as his team's chances at next year's championship.

He picked up his books and pencil case, and hiked his stick onto his shoulder. The boys crossed the boulevard to the sidewalk. The grass was yellow and matted, the mud wet and slimy underfoot. Paul seemed to have turned on a talking switch. "Sawchuk is the best there is right now," he said. "He was brilliant when he stopped Bernie Geoffrion's boomers, wasn't he?"

Dale's life was wrapped up in hockey. His love for the Detroit Red Wings kept him glued to the radio and reading the sports pages in the newspaper every day. Hockey was his passion, and certainly his escape when he felt sad. He was sad now, but hockey wasn't first in his thoughts.

Paul was usually a Boston Bruins fan, but when they didn't make the playoffs, he switched his allegiance to Detroit. "I couldn't believe Montreal won the last game. Boom Boom's slapshot is great," Paul continued, talking to himself as they walked. He stepped over a shiny patch of old, dirty ice. "But Montreal's in trouble, especially since Detroit has Gordie Howe. I think he'll score big for the Red Wings tonight." Paul swung his pail some more.

The rattling noise reverberated in Dale's head. "Nothing could be better than to have the series tied at three-all."

They reached the corner of the street and crossed over. There were more mounds of snow on the boulevards and grass, but only a few edges left on the curbs. Paul crunched his boot against one.

The handle on Dale's pail dug into his fingers. He pressed it against his body, wrapping his hand around it. He had a little bit of homework—a few mathematics problems, a paragraph to translate into Latin, and some French questions. He had to start work on an essay about the history of science, too. He'd been putting it off, chalking up the delay to his hockey playoffs, but really, he was being lazy. Usually, he'd try to get his work done before supper, but he had to get the table set, too, and today, all he wanted to do was lie down. He'd been looking forward to tonight's game, but the lousier he felt, the more his spirits slumped.

"All I know is our Winnipeg boy has a chance to win the Cup tonight," Paul said. "Now that *Moh-reese Ree-shard* isn't there—" he stretched out the pronunciation of Montreal player Maurice Richard's French name "—so much the better for Sawchuk!"

Dale didn't want to talk, and pretended his world hadn't been rocked. "Yeah, too bad about the fight at the game in March. I was surprised when the NHL suspended Richard for the rest of the season, and then the playoffs, too. That's tough for Montreal." He grew warm in his jacket, then a chill made him shiver. He did up one button but, almost immediately, his feet began to sweat in his boots. Only a few more houses until he could rest.

"I'll bet Sawchuk's family over in Elmwood will be sitting around the radio," Paul babbled. "Or maybe one of them has a television already. Detroit beat Montreal last year with Sawchuk in net. If he wins tonight, there'll be celebrating across the river."

"All over Canada, since all the players on the Red Wings are Canadian, anyway. For sure, all over Winnipeg," Dale said.

"Remember, you might be a goalie for Detroit one day, too." Paul elbowed Dale as they walked.

"Hmph," Dale said, nodding at his house as they approached it. "Not with the way my dad's acting. I can hardly practice any more since my mom died. He's always calling me inside to take care of Brent, and he has a list of jobs he wants done, but the list never gets shorter. What about what I want to do?"

His family's bungalow looked welcoming, like all the other homes on the tree-lined street. The wooden siding showed some chips in the white paint, so Dale assumed he'd be assigned to sand those areas down and paint them during the summer holidays. He looked at everything in his house now with a view to wondering what work needed to be done. The storm windows had accumulated a layer of film after the long winter, but in a few days, they'd be able to lift the wooden sash at the bottom and let fresh air flow through the air holes. Soon, the summer screens would replace the storm windows entirely. He should have felt happy about the prospect of warmer weather, yet a bad feeling rose up inside of him.

"I get it," Paul said. "I'll bet it's been hard." He kicked at a remnant of ice. "Listen, Dale. Sorry I had to tell you—about leaving. It's been ... hard."

"I get it, too," Dale said. He shifted his pail and sighed. "I gotta go in now. See you later." He wanted to dash away, but he had no energy to run.

"Thanks," Paul smiled, shaking the pail again. "I

knew you'd understand. Hey, it's gonna be a great game! We'll talk about it tomorrow." He carried on down the street, the sound of the pail still annoying Dale. He turned up the sidewalk to his house.

Suddenly, his stomach heaved and bile rose into his throat. He choked it back. *Maybe I'm turning into Glenn Hall*, Dale thought, putting his own pail down on the verandah to wait for tomorrow's practice. He opened the screen door and went inside with his books, which also seemed to be getting heavier as the minutes passed.

CHAPTER 3

"Hello, Canada, and hockey fans in the United States and Newfoundland."

The voice crackled through the cloth-covered speaker. Dale knew people were huddled around radios all over the country, and if they were lucky enough, staring at the screens of their new television sets. He thought it would be terrific to actually see the players as they skated, not just listen to the play-by-play description. Paul was so lucky to have a television in his family. Maybe Dad would hear from other people how exciting it was, and want one, too. Maybe next year. Dad had other things on his mind right now.

"Welcome to the third period of the final game of the Stanley Cup series, between the Montreal Canadiens and the Detroit Red Wings, on this Wednesday, April 14th, 1955. This is Foster Hewitt, speaking to you from The Old Red Barn—the Olympia Stadium in downtown Detroit,

Michigan. The series is tied, but so far in this game, it's 2-0 for Detroit, with Alex Delvecchio hitting the net at 7:12 into the second period to open the scoring—his sixth of the playoffs. Then Number 9, Gordie Howe, secured the second at 19:49 with an assist by Marcel Pronovost. Montreal will have to fight hard to turn things around," Hewitt intoned. "The teams are returning from the dressing room; the players are lining up on the benches."

"Turn it up," Brent demanded. "I can't hear." The six-year-old scrambled to his knees on the area rug in the living room, and put his ear up to the speaker. He tried to wrap his arms around the big wooden console, but they were too short and could only reach the edges.

"Move away, squirt! You're blocking the sound," Dale complained. He was slumped in the corner of the red chesterfield. He still felt awful, but had managed to finish most of his homework. He decided to leave his essay until right before bed. They were studying biology in science class. The teacher had given them a few optional topics, and he'd chosen to write about Gregor Mendel, the Austrian monk who developed the first understanding of genetics in the 1800s by studying generations of pea plants.

Working later into the night was easier than getting up early to do his assignments. Luckily, he didn't have to share a bedroom with his brother, whose bedtime, except for tonight, was 8 PM. But now he was wondering if he could push himself to stay up tonight. He usually used the time before bed to write about his day in a diary his mother had given him as a birthday present, a few years earlier.

When he was little, Dale had watched his mother as she took a moment every afternoon to get a black hard-covered book out of her night-table drawer, then go off by herself into the living room. She'd settle into the chair—the one his dad used now to read the paper— then she'd open the book to a blank, lined page, and take the top off her fountain pen. She'd breathe out before beginning to write—sometimes writing only a little, sometimes furiously filling the page, either smiling or furrowing her brow, before capping the pen, closing the cover, and returning it to the night-table drawer. Then she got back to her work. She never shared what she'd written, but it seemed to be an extension of her. She always seemed content when she was done.

He'd snuck into her room a few times to peek inside

the book, but he could only decipher printed letters then, and she wrote in cursive script. When he was older and could finally read, he felt wary of snooping into her private thoughts, and decided against it.

When she gave him a blank book of his own—a blue scribbler, really—he asked what he should write. "Anything you want," she said. "That's for you to decide. What do you think about?"

The decision was easy. Hockey consumed his thoughts, so he wrote about hockey. He found it useful to analyze his plays by describing in ink what he had done, a new page for every entry. Sometimes he made sketches of the plays. If a shot got by him, he wrote out how he should have moved to keep the puck out of the net, then drew a picture of the action, with arrows showing him what he should have done. He read the diary entries over and memorized his instructions, so he could practice them out on the rink with Paul. He found the process helped him.

Leonard came at me from the right. I guessed his speed, but I should have checked the angle of his shoulder, and the way he dug in with his elbow to force the shot—he's trying *something new. I thought he would pass, but he bore down and slapped it past me. Next time, I've got to twist my body to the left, swing my hips to the right, and turn my skates to the side to stop the puck. My arms have to fly out to put them off their shot. I have to pay attention to keeping my left arm high, in case he passes it. ***I have to keep better track of each player, too. They all have their tricks!****

The diary was good therapy, especially after a loss. He'd tried to use it for that purpose after his mother died, but he couldn't draw anything positive out of that terrible night.

I still can't believe it. Did she know she was sick? Why did she die? Could I have done anything? Dad's stuck, and so are we. I don't know what to do.

He was surprised at how brief those entries were, how he didn't want to remember the play-by-play of what he saw. His hand slowed as he wrote, and finally stopped moving. Trying to make sense of it upset him all over again, and no amount of writing would bring her back.

He knew he'd be too tired to write tonight, and what would he write about his best friend's announcement, anyway? Another disaster he couldn't explain to himself, or didn't want to. Was it his fault for being better than Paul?

Maybe it was Paul's announcement that had ruined his appetite at supper. He'd dabbled with his mashed potatoes, the way he'd done when he was little, finally scooping them up together with a spoonful of creamed corn, but not much else. He hadn't touched his meatloaf at all. Leftover from the night before, it looked dry after being warmed over in the oven. Dad didn't have Mom's deft touch at cooking. Dale thought about learning to cook himself, so they would have decent meals, at least once in a while.

Despite not eating, he didn't feel hungry.

His grandmother had come over for several weeks after his mom died, bringing dishes Dale loved—meatballs, roast beef, fried fish with hash browns—but she broke into tears every so often, especially when she talked about "my Grace," confusing Brent and upsetting Dad. The last time Grandma cried was as they were finishing supper. Dad asked the boys to leave the table.

Dale couldn't make out much of their conversation, only at one point hearing Grandma say, "I lost my daughter," and Dad shushing her. Grandma stopped coming over after that.

"Turn it up," Brent demanded again.

Dale shook himself back into consciousness. "It's as loud as it can be. Move away from the radio, already." He lifted his shoulders to try and relieve the throbbing in his back.

The voice crackled, "He scores! It's Alex Delvecchio, shooting it in, unassisted at two minutes, fifty-nine seconds in the final period. He's got the insurance goal!" The crowd noise filled the living room.

"We're winning!" Brent squealed, bounding up and down as he clutched the radio. "The real, real Alexander the Great got the goal—not our Alexander," he said, trying to muddle through the explanation in his mind. "You know what I mean, right?"

Dale nodded. "I get it, squirt. Paul won't be offended." He couldn't help but smile at Brent. "You're sure you'd rather be a fan than a player?"

Brent wrinkled his nose. "Nah, I tried it. Skating's just for fun. I like to listen to the games or watch when you play." He pressed his ear harder to the radio speaker.

"You could be good," Dale reminded him, trying to sound cheery to mask his discomfort. It was the final game of the hockey playoffs. He should be enthusiastic.

"Nah." Brent tried to work his body even closer to the radio, his smile stretching across his face.

"Move back, for goodness sake, Brent." Dad stood in the doorway to the kitchen. He'd fetched the newspaper and made himself a cup of tea during the break. "We all want to hear the game."

Brent's smile disappeared. "Okay, okay," he said, dropping his arms from the radio console and scurrying back, careful not to disturb his collection of four hockey cards, carefully arranged on the carpet. He'd bought the chalky, cardboard-like bubble gum packs with money he'd received for his birthday. The awful gum lasted only a few minutes, before becoming hard and impossible to chew, but kids bought it to collect and trade the images of sports heroes in each pack.

Brent took his job as a fan seriously. His cards were of players of teams other than Detroit, but he studied their statistics anyway, mispronouncing words as he tried to figure them out. He crossed his legs, tucked his elbows into his knees, plunked his chin on his wrists, and fixed his eyes on the radio, waiting for the announcer to describe the face-off. Dale could see Brent picturing the plays in his head.

"You'll need to check the drainpipe from the roof tomorrow, Dale, so we don't get water in the basement from the snowmelt," his father said. He folded himself into the reading chair across from the radio, setting the cup and saucer on the round wooden table beside him. He tugged at the knee of his trousers and laid the newspaper on his legs. "I'll check on the window wells, make sure there's no ice there." Dale didn't answer. The list never ended, even on the last game of the Stanley Cup series.

Then Dad turned his attention to the game. "Looks like Montreal is finished. Hmph." He took a sip of tea, returned the cup to the saucer, and picked up the paper. As he read the front page, he traced his fingers along his jaw, back and forth, back and forth, something Dale noticed him doing a lot lately. Dad had also been sobbing in his bedroom in the middle of the night since his mom died, but Dale knew he would never confess to his sons that he was grieving. When Brent asked him about the black circles under his eyes some mornings, Dad's response was what Dale expected: "Nothing's wrong. Finish your breakfast," and he'd gone off to work.

His dad seemed lost in thought now, thumbing *The Winnipeg Tribune* and pulling out the sports pages. Looking at the paper while he spoke, he asked Dale, "Do you think Montreal can win without Maurice Richard?"

"I think Terry Sawchuk is so good, it won't make a difference," Dale said. He shifted his position on the couch again, sitting slightly straighter. Now his shoulders ached, too.

Foster Hewitt continued, "... and Montreal, the league's oldest club ..." Then suddenly he shouted, "With five and a half minutes left in the game, Sawchuk loses his stick! And Montreal's Floyd Curry whacks in the rebound to score! Is Montreal still in the game? Can they turn it around?"

"Whoa," Brent exclaimed from the floor. "Did you hear that?" He turned from his father to his brother, a huge smile on his face, his eyes dancing. He slapped his palms on his knees and settled back down to listen.

"Don't worry," Dale said, shifting himself again. "Sawchuk will hold them." He held his breath for a moment, then called over to his father. "Do you think I could be as good as Terry Sawchuk one day, Dad?"

Their father snapped the newspaper in half and, without raising his eyes, said, "Things have changed, Dale. You'd better get used to it. You know I need you here at home now. I doubt you'll be able to play hockey next year."

Dale pinched his thumb and index finger together, squeezing to create pressure, so he could avoid thinking about what his father had just said. But he had known it was coming. Their lives had been turned upside down since his mother's death in January. Right after she died, his father quit his job at the railway to take a position as a mechanic at the Roco gas station, right at the top of Smithfield Avenue at Main Street, only a few blocks away. He earned less, but he could walk to work for 8 AM, instead of leaving at 6:30 to catch the streetcar to the train station, and a feeder train out to the railway yards. The boys were home from school only a few minutes before their dad arrived back, too.

Dad said he liked his new job. He realized he had a talent for figuring out each car's problem, and talked about one day owning one himself—he favored the two-tone dark green and light green Chevrolet Bel Air. But he grumbled that his new job paid less than the railway, and complained about the added housework on top of the chores he'd always done. Several times, he suggested Dale should now chip in on an equal basis.

It was all to take care of Brent, even though neither his dad nor he really paid much attention to playing with the little boy—walking him to the library, or listening to his prattle, singing goofy nursery rhymes and songs from the radio, the way his mom did. Dad and Dale were always working. The three of them ate together, but their suppers were short and silent, followed by homework or chores. The playoffs had proven to be a brief respite, but Dale could tell his father was thinking about jobs that needed doing, rather than really listening to the broadcasts.

Dale's last season had been so strong that he dared to imagine himself suiting up in a clean new NHL jersey one day, not the faded, holey sweater a generation of goalies had worn before him at the Perth Community Center. Every spring, those uniforms were folded and stored in cardboard boxes. The coach tossed in naphthalene mothballs to deter moth larvae from munching on the material during the hot summer, so many mothballs that the sickly-sweet smell overwhelmed the storage closet where they were kept. But every September, some of the sweaters had holes in them, anyway. Dale's mom had laughed last year when he brought home his goalie jersey.

"Look how well fed those moths are," she said, holding up Dale's sweater with the number 3 attached. Dale counted more than a dozen holes, making them even larger whenever he poked his finger through. His mom picked up the slipped stitches with a needle and sewed the holes shut, giving Dale a wink when he said, "Thanks, Mom."

His mother still seemed healthy then.

Every September, the coach's wife laundered all the sweaters. One washing was never enough to get rid of the telltale odor, though. Dale and Paul would sometimes bike over on sunny autumn Sundays, and help Mr. Leah air them out along the boards of the skating rink.

The players' moms had to wash the sweaters several times, before the boys could stick their noses into the material without the smell overpowering them. "Any better?" Mr. Leah chuckled at the scrunched expressions on the boys' faces.

Dale had also imagined that one day, he would own brand new skates that fit properly. The well-worn pair of hand-me-downs dangling on the nail in his basement had to be padded with extra socks, so his feet wouldn't move inside the boot. Polished, sturdy leather to support his ankles, sharp blades, shiny instead of rust-spotted—that would be a dream come true. What would his dad's edict mean for his dream to make an NHL team?

Maybe the news of Paul's leaving would change Dad's mind, make him see that now, Dale had a clear shot at being a standout as well as a starter, that the team needed him.

"Paul's moving, Dad. He's going to be the starter for Northwood next year," Dale said. Dad put down his paper, and Dale told him all about it. His fatigue was growing. The conversation and the blathering from the radio were wearing him down.

"Really? Well, too bad he's going, but my mind's pretty well made up," his dad said, returning to his newspaper. He rubbed his fingers along his jaw again.

Brent, who had been staring at the radio, had been listening all along. He piped up, "Are you mad at Paul? Why didn't he come tonight?"

The Detroit crowd exploded. Another save. Dale sat up, trying not to show he felt shattered, trying not to show how sick he was, trying to pretend he was still excited about the game, when actually a dull roar inside his head muffled all the sounds together.

"Three minutes left in the third period. The Detroit Red Wings are poised to win ..."

"He's at his grandparents'," Dale answered. The impact of Paul's decision was now settling in. Dale had to figure out if he was jealous at having a rival, sad at losing a friend, or maybe both. But if Dad took Dale out of hockey, the basis for their friendship would surely end.

He was too tired to think about the conundrum. He would have gone to sleep early, except for the game. Then his father wouldn't have had the opportunity to make his pronouncement. He tried to focus on the action.

"One minute remaining, and there's a time out ..."

Brent hooted. Then he blurted out, "Oh, yeah—Dad, I have a paper for you to sign. We're going to get a polio needle at school next week. I have to give the paper back to my teacher."

While the players scrummed, Brent ran to the hall closet and rummaged in his coat pocket, pulling out a folded paper. Dad opened it up and studied the information. "Hmph," he said, frowning. "What do they know?" He put the paper down beside his teacup.

"What do you mean?" Dale asked. "It was front page news on Monday. There's a vaccine now, so kids won't get polio anymore. You read about it," he said, pointing at the *Tribune*. "Summer's coming, and it's always worse then. That's why they're giving little kids like Brent the needles at school."

His dad waved his hand at the newspaper. "The bout in '53 was a bad one, but hardly anyone got sick last summer, so why get a needle now? Who says it will happen again? Maybe it won't."

"What do you mean?"

"You can't trust doctors, Dale. What do they know, anyway? They want to make money, that's all." His dad leaned back in his chair. "I heard what Walter Winchell said last year, that they were stockpiling white coffins for little kids because the vaccine didn't work."

"That was bunk, Dad." Dale couldn't believe that his father, who read the paper every night, accepted the word of a gossip columnist on a radio show. "You know Winchell made it up."

"Who said he made it up? The government? What do they know?"

Dale was exasperated. "Yes, the government, yes, the doctors—they know. They proved the vaccine works. I don't get why you think a guy with a microphone and a fifteen-minute radio show knows more. What kind of expert is he?"

"Hmph," Dad snorted, running his finger along the edge of his saucer. He imitated Winchell's machine-gun delivery. *"Good evening, Mr. and Mrs. North and South America and all the ships at sea ... let's go to press!"* Then he became himself again. "You have to listen hard to him, he speaks so fast. He's funny, too."

"So what?" Dale did not want to be talking about this now. He wanted to be in bed. "He's an expert about which movie stars are getting married and divorced, and what fancy clothes they're wearing."

"But he might be right," Dad said. "What if the government really is collecting coffins, because they know the vaccine doesn't work? You never know."

"No one's found any piles of coffins, Dad. Remember? All made up. Bunk! He's trying to scare people, so they'll listen to his show. You need to make sure Brent gets vaccinated."

His father ignored Dale's rebuke. "Never mind. My

grandfather got sick when I was a kid. I remember it all like it was yesterday. The doctor at the hospital operated on him, but he died anyway, and my grandmother still had to pay the bill. All that money for nothing! My dad learned a lesson right then." Dad rubbed his jaw. "So, when I got scarlet fever, he and my mother wouldn't let the doctor put me in the hospital—they didn't have the cash, and what was it going to accomplish? They kept me in a room by myself and I got over it." He took another sip of tea and carefully replaced the cup on the saucer. "I got over it."

Dale had heard this story a thousand times. It had never made sense to him, even when he was younger, but his father would never admit his statement was illogical. Dale's energy was ebbing. "You told me other kids developed heart problems from scarlet fever," he reminded his father. "You were just lucky."

"Yeah, and most people are lucky, without lining other people's pockets. Tell your teacher you don't need it, Brent," Dad said, signaling the end of the discussion.

Brent shrugged his shoulders from the center of the carpet. "All the other kids are getting it," he said.

"Well, you're not 'other kids,'" his dad said, closing

the newspaper and slapping it on his leg. "Now listen to the game."

"But—"

"We're done with this," Dad ordered, his forehead knitted. "Don't I have enough to do around here without you bothering me about nothing?"

Brent shrunk. "Okay, Dad. Okay."

"But, Dad," Dale said. He curled back into the couch. He wanted to go to bed. Didn't his father see he was sick, that he wasn't shouting and screaming in front of the radio, like he usually did when a game was being broadcast? "No doctors are making any money off this. Come on, I know you read about it." He pointed at *The Tribune* again. "The government is giving the vaccine free to every little kid in Canada, and they're doing the same in the States, to make sure they don't get paralyzed or have to live in iron lungs. Why wouldn't you want him to get it? You don't want him to end up in the hospital! What if there's another epidemic?"

He added, "Mom would have signed it."

Dad shut his eyes and pinched the bridge of his nose. Behind them, Foster Hewitt babbled excitedly, but there was a stillness in the air of the living room at 121 Smithfield. "Yes," his father said after a moment, opening his eyes. He reached out and swiveled the handle of the teacup with his index finger. "Yes, but I'm not Mom, so let's not argue."

"... The Detroit Red Wings win the Stanley Cup! The final score is 3-1. For the second straight year, these colorful, well-matched teams went down to the seventh game ..."

Dale knew that all over Canada, all over Winnipeg, across the river in Elmwood, people were celebrating the win, celebrating the many players who came from their communities. He knew they should be celebrating Terry Sawchuk, their hometown hero.

But neither Dale, Brent, nor their dad joined the country in its joy. They sat there, looking at the radio, each of them numb.

"This is Foster Hewitt, signing off for another year."

"Time for bed. I've got to load some coal into the furnace," Dad said quietly. "Brent, go brush your teeth." He stood up and headed for the basement door in the hallway.

Dale wanted to apologize to his dad, for making him feel bad. His remark had re-opened the gulf that had been growing between them.

He was about to speak, when a searing hot pain ripped up his legs, into his back, and raced like lightning through his chest, its violence nearly throwing Dale off the couch.

"Dad," he gasped, his eyes bulging and fear gripping his heart. "Help me!"

CHAPTER 4

"We're going to open this up later," Dr. Barsky said. He stood to the side of Dale's head, his hand resting on the giant respirator that had heaved relentlessly against Dale's chest for the past week, forcing him to draw air in and then push it out.

This morning, the orderlies had rolled him in his iron lung from another room on the same floor to a new ward for boys, some in iron lungs, some in beds. "You're out of the isolation unit now—a good first step. Now, try and plan how you're going to breathe without the iron lung. We'll keep our eyes on your lips and nails to see if they turn blue or stay pink. See you later," Dr. Barsky said. He smiled, tapped the machine, and headed over to another patient.

Polio. No one had said it directly to him, or maybe they had. He'd been too sick to be conscious of what was happening. But he knew. The epidemics swept the country randomly, mostly in summer months. He'd heard and seen the horror stories. A few kids in his neighborhood had contracted it. Two years earlier, both kids and the mother in the Palmer family one street over had gotten sick. The nine-year-old, Harvey, recovered, but Linda, only a toddler, died, and Mrs. Palmer was paralyzed—forever. Dale had seen her husband carrying her to a lawn chair on nice days. She couldn't lift a hand to do anything for herself—not even sip from a glass, feed herself, or even scratch her nose.

Children were forbidden from going near that house, because their parents were afraid they could catch polio. Harvey sat on the steps of his house, by himself, now an eleven-year-old, never in the company of other children.

A lot of parents wouldn't let their kids go swimming outdoors at Pritchard Pool, as they had every summer for as long as anyone could remember. They kept them out of theaters and other places, where kids gathered in numbers, because they were afraid someone would transfer polio germs. Everyone's mother scrubbed and scoured their homes from top to bottom, fearful the polio virus might have entered the house, even washing fruit and vegetables from the grocery store with soap and water. Dale's parents were no different in worrying about the danger facing their children. They tried to get him and Brent to nap every afternoon to "preserve their strength," but Dale balked at the suggestion, and even Brent, who was only four years old at the time, rebelled at being treated like a baby. Mom and Dad did keep them at home, though, and made sure they got a thorough bathing every night.

"You can play with Brent," his mother had told Dale when he wanted to meet his friends. She would not listen to a word of opposition, so Dale played ball hockey with his brother in their yard. Scrimmaging with a much smaller boy wasn't much of a challenge for a skilled player, but Dale remembered how being indulged by older, better players had helped him. Brent was starting even earlier than he had, and Dale was immediately struck by Brent's uncanny ability to imagine other players on the ice, and a variety of ways to steal the puck.

"Maybe I'll be a hockey player, too," Brent said. He ran circles around Dale, showing big-kid swagger, snagging the ball, and knocking it past the wooden chair that served as a goal post. "He scores!" Brent raised his arms, delighted in his triumph over his older brother.

Their mother rewarded them with gallons of sugary, raspberry-flavored Kool-Aid to quench their thirst after their backyard battles.

They played for hours, with breaks for tickling and nonsense. For more diversion, they scrounged for chunks of coal that bounced off the big delivery trucks rumbling down the back lanes, delivering fuel to households for the coming fall and winter. Brent tossed them in the air and Dale smacked them as far as he could with the blade of his stick. They turned their isolation into fun.

At least he didn't suffer the way Paul did. Every day for several weeks, Paul's older sisters made him play school at a makeshift desk they'd set up in their basement. "The basement's nice and cool," Paul told Dale, "but my sisters make me do schoolwork. I have to stand at attention and sing 'O Canada' in the morning, and then 'God Save the Queen' at the end of the day."

"What? That's ridiculous!"

"And then they make me sing more songs, like 'O Shenandoah,' in the dumb music classes they make up. I had to write an essay and do arithmetic, too. They boss me around all the time. Ugh."

A few parents sent their kids to stay with relatives on farms, with the idea that being away from the city and other kids would keep them safe. Others made their son or daughter wear garlic on a string around their neck in the hottest months, hoping the smell would ward off the virus. One of those kids got polio, anyway. The summer of 1953 had been the worst, with Winnipeg hospitals filling up and too many kids dying.

Some towns kept the schools closed, until the weather cooled in the fall, when the spread of the virus seemed to slow.

Dale had seen others get sick, but it never occurred to him that he might become a victim, might not be able to lift a finger to help himself, eat on his own, sip from a glass, or scratch his own nose.

When he'd awakened in the iron lung, he'd been terrified to realize what he had, terrified that air was being sucked in through a tube in his throat, terrified of the noise and power of the machine that controlled his existence, terrified of the pain that ratcheted through his arms and legs, and he was unable to control it. He was terrified of all the people in white masks who worked on him without acknowledging him. They flipped a switch that produced an eerie light inside the iron lung, so they could see as they poked at him, sticking their arms through the portholes to turn him or wrap his arms and legs in hot, itchy wool cloth to loosen his muscles. His skin screamed at the heat, but no one paid attention to his coughs or choking sounds of objection.

The tracheotomy tube had been removed after a few days, a frightening few minutes. As he withdrew the tube, though, Dr. Barsky spoke in reassuring tones, encouraging Dale to relax. He began with, "Your dad says you're a pretty good goalie," and he talked about his own love of hockey—his team of choice was the Toronto Maple Leafs. Tim Horton and Ted Kennedy were his favorite players, and before Dale knew it, the tube was out, the pressure in his neck suddenly relieved. Dr. Barsky covered the hole quickly with a gauze dressing and secured the pad with adhesive tape. "We'll watch that, Dale. If you lie still, it should close on its own and you won't need stitches."

How could he do anything but lie still? He was paralyzed in a hospital. His mother had died in one, only a few months earlier. In the middle of the night, he'd been woken by the voices of his father and two men. He'd opened his bedroom door to see his mother lying on a stretcher, pale and unmoving, being wheeled out the door. His father, who'd obviously thrown on rumpled pants and a shirt, was pulling his overcoat off the hanger when he saw Dale. At that moment, Mrs. Winocur, their next-door neighbor, tumbled through the doorway, wrapped in her winter coat, her hair a-jumble.

"Go," she said to his dad. "I'll stay with them."

Dad shoved his arm into his coat. "Mom's sick. Help get Brent to school if I'm not back in the morning." Then he ran out the door to the ambulance.

When Dale woke up in the morning, Mrs. Winocur was gone. His dad sat at the kitchen table, swirling a spoon in the coffee cup in front of him. His hair was disheveled. His coat lay across the chair beside him.

"Your mother won't be coming home," he muttered without raising his eyes. "She had a heart attack. She's dead."

That was it. The family had stumbled on since then.

Now, a new black Bakelite telephone sat on the kitchen counter, with the phone number 59-0744 penciled in the center of the dial. Dale recalled his parents discussing the value of having one, with Mom suggesting she could make appointments, call her mother, or "What if there's an emergency?" she'd said.

But Dad had balked at the cost. "Three dollars and thirty-nine cents—every month? We can't afford that," he said.

That was why it took a few extra minutes for the ambulance to arrive. When Dad cried in the night, Dale heard him curse himself for the time it had taken to run over to the Winocurs' house and bang on the door, until they woke up and let him in to call for help.

Several times, Dale saw Brent playing with the phone, sticking his finger into the holes and dragging the dial down to the stop position, again and again. Otherwise, the new gadget sat mostly mute.

Dale tried not to think about his mom and what had happened to her in a hospital. At least, he wasn't going to die, it seemed. He tried not to think about hockey, either, but he couldn't help it. Would he be left with a body that didn't work? Would he ever play again? Would his father change his mind and let him?

He didn't want to risk having stitches in his throat,

so instead of turning his head, he whisked his eyes right and left, the way he did as a goalie, when he tracked the lightning movements of the puck, so he could pounce if it came near his crease. On either side of him, he saw that iron lungs held the bodies of boys of different ages, all of them looking up at the white, boring ceiling. Nurses in their starched white uniforms and starched white caps bustled about. They were always talking—to patients, yes—but mostly to each other. The orderlies and nurses' aides were similarly clad in white, but with no hats. They were also busy, some reaching inside the portholes, looking as if they were on treasure hunts. Some pushed metal carts with stacks of white linens, the wheels clattering on the linoleum floor. Others walked by, carrying silver pans covered with a single white towel. All of them talking, acting as if a room full of helpless, imprisoned children was normal.

He cleared his throat—hesitantly and carefully—and this time it hurt less. But his nose needed a blow, and he couldn't do it for himself. His arms lay useless in the iron lung; when he tried to move his limbs, pain ricocheted up, down, and across.

A nurse walked by. "Can you help me?" Dale called

out in as strong a voice as he could muster. "My nose—it's running."

"I'm busy," she said, a sharp tone in her voice, only slowing down long enough to deny him. "Can't you see?" She carried a pair of rumpled pajamas. "I'll get to you later." She walked quickly away.

A single tear leaked from each of Dale's eyes, trickling along his temples, soaking into his hair.

Suddenly, a tissue appeared from the side, encircling his nose and blocking his vision. "Blow," said a girl's voice. Dale didn't know what to do. "Blow," the voice above the tissue ordered again. Dale could not help but do what she commanded, his nose felt so full. She finished wiping his nose and turned away to throw the tissue into the small wastebasket under his iron lung.

When she turned back, Dale's heart skipped a beat. He flicked his eyes as far as possible to the right to see her. The girl was about his age, her shiny black hair drawn back in a ponytail, her big brown eyes sparkling. Her face was at the height of his head. She wore blue plaid flannel pajamas, with a gray housecoat bundled around her. Her hands moved her wheelchair back and forth. She smiled at him, showing off beautiful white teeth that made her eyes sparkle more.

"Uh ..." Dale stuttered. He had never been in such a situation. "Thanks," he said.

"My pleasure," she said, shrugging her shoulders. "Don't get rattled by people like Miss Clements." She raised her chin to indicate the unpleasant nurse, now at the other end of the room. "Everyone needs help, so sometimes the nurses and orderlies get crabby. And some people—like her—maybe should get different jobs." She rolled her chair back and forth again. "Anyway, people helped me out, so now I do what I can. Keeps me busy."

Again, Dale didn't know what to say. The girl's smile made her cheeks round and rosy, and made him feel brighter, happier. "Thanks," he said again.

"I was in one of those metal tubes, too, you know, for three months," the girl said. "You'll probably get out of it. You'll see. I'm Charlene Arcand. What's your name?"

He introduced himself. "How long have you been here?" Dale gasped the words out. This was the most he'd spoken since he'd regained consciousness. She was more advanced in her recovery, but he needed to know what that meant in terms of time.

"I got sick last June, nearly eleven months ago," Charlene said, leaning forward on the armrests of her wheelchair. "It seems like a long time, but some kids have been here longer."

Dale felt himself break out in goosebumps inside the iron lung. The thought of being confined in this machine for any length of time scared him. But this girl had been in an iron lung for three long months, and after nearly a year, had only progressed to sitting in a wheelchair. He looked at her—nearly a year in pajamas! Despite looking so serious as she spoke, she looked happy—and beautiful.

Hockey practices were set to begin right after Halloween, when the rinks at the community centers would be flooded. It was already near the end of April. He needed to be better to start the season in goal.

Dale looked up at the ceiling before asking his question. "Does everyone get better?" Suddenly, he couldn't remember anything he'd learned about how people had recovered from polio. His heart raced.

"You never know," Charlene said. "Everybody's different. Most kids go home, so maybe you'll be out of here soon. You're the new kid who plays hockey, aren't you?"

"How did you know?" Dale asked, his eyes straining

to the right to get a really good look at her. He had just met Charlene. He hadn't mentioned anything about himself. She sat back in her chair.

"Oh, everybody talks about everybody else here," she said. "That's all we have to do." She leaned her chin on her left hand. "You should meet George, then. He plays—well, he *played*—hockey, too. Quite a hotshot, he was. At least that's what he says."

Dr. Barsky approached, followed by two orderlies, who stationed themselves beside Dale's head. They placed their hands on the latches, ready to open the metal clasps holding the giant cylinder closed.

"Time to see how you can do without this contraption, Dale. Charlene," he asked, looking over at her. "Will you excuse us for now?"

"Sure," Charlene said. "I have to get back to my ward," she said, swinging the chair around but calling back to Dale. "I'll come back tomorrow, okay? I'll bring George, too."

"Sure!" Dale brightened up. "Sure." His thoughts swirled and his heart pumped faster. He watched her ponytail bounce along as she wheeled away. He realized how good it felt to talk to someone his age—even though it wasn't about hockey. Maybe tomorrow he'd find another friend in George.

Dr. Barsky set up a divider around Dale's head, the soft pleats in the white cloth curtain obscuring what would take place inside it. The first time he'd seen a divider had been when he lay on the gurney in the emergency department. The doctor there had set one up around him. He'd shifted Dale onto his side and moved his legs up, so he lay in a fetal position, his back rounded to separate the vertebrae for the spinal tap—the test to confirm a polio diagnosis. Dale had gasped at the pain of bending, and from fright, because his breathing was quickly becoming labored. His father had blanched at the sight of the syringe.

"There's nothing wrong with him," he'd heard his father mumble. "He's a hockey player. He's tired from the playoffs, that's all. He'll be fine."

The doctor had looked at Dad with wide eyes, wrinkling his brow. "Perhaps you should wait outside, sir," he'd said, adjusting his face mask and motioning Dad to the other side of the divider. His father had disappeared. Dale could hear people talking all over the emergency department, calling and shouting.

He'd winced when the needle pierced his skin, the long thin metal feeling more like a wooden stake being driven into the space between his vertebrae. He'd felt a sucking sensation as the doctor drew back the plunger, the fluid from inside his spine streaming into the barrel of the syringe. He'd thought he was holding his breath to keep still, but quickly realized that no air was coming into his lungs. The doctor had applied a bandage over the wound in his back. Dale had tried again to inhale, but instead, only a gurgling sound came out of his throat. Suddenly, the shouting was coming from inside his own cubicle—the doctor hollering loudly for assistance—immediately.

The next thing he remembered was waking up in the iron lung.

Now, behind this divider, Dr. Barsky was threatening to turn off the electricity. At least Dale could breathe inside the lung. The intense pain in his legs and back was constant; now he was being threatened with the inability to breathe.

Fear overtook him. In the next year or so, scouts

would be coming to games to evaluate him. He couldn't afford to be in the hospital for as long as Charlene. He had worked too hard to get his position on the team. He could and would apply the same determination and effort to getting over this. It would be worth it to accomplish his dream.

What should he do and how could he do it? Most of all, where was his father?

The silence and the click happened simultaneously—a terror-filled moment, followed by a pull as Dr. Barsky drew the front of the machine forward. His neck was still circled by the collar, but the bed rolled out of the machine, exposing Dale to a world that now frightened him. Followed by ... a breath—his breath, a stuttering, stumbling breath, followed by another, and another. Dale watched Dr. Barsky and the orderlies standing close by, all of them focusing on his lips and fingernails to check their color, his chest to see if it expanded, then back to his lips and fingernails. They all stood at the ready.

"Good, good," the doctor observed, as Dale mustered all his energy to inflate his lungs, consciously trying to do what should be instinct, breathing in, breathing out.

"Good, good, keep going." Dale responded and, for a brief moment, thought he could feel more pleasure than pain.

"Wonderful," Dr. Barsky exclaimed, a smile spreading across his face, his eyes twinkling behind his glasses. "You moved your wrist, Dale," he said. "You moved your wrist!"

The orderlies laughed. "Well done," one of them said. The other patted Dale on the arm. "You'll be up and out of here soon, son."

"But not yet. That's enough for now." Dr. Barsky didn't have to say another word. He pushed the bed forward. The orderlies worked swiftly, closing Dale back into the iron lung and sealing the latches. One flipped the switch, energizing the leather bellows underneath the bed. Dale felt the vibration as it began to throb again, exercising pressure on his chest so he would draw oxygen in and push carbon dioxide out. If he could have, Dale would have collapsed. He was exhausted.

"You did well, Dale," Dr. Barsky said. "We'll try again tomorrow for a longer time, and soon, who knows, maybe you'll skate away from us." He smiled and Dale smiled, too. From the other side of the divider, voices called out, "Good for you!" "Congratulations!" "I knew you could do it!" Dale could feel his heart beating.

"Tomorrow is Sunday, visiting day. Your dad will be here," Dr. Barsky said. Inside the iron lung, Dale gasped in happiness.

CHAPTER 5

Dale had hardly slept the night before, he'd been so charged by his accomplishment when the iron lung had been opened. Overnight, more strength returned to his body. He'd spent the evening moving his wrist, so pleased that his hand moved back and forth. He was certain he could fold his palm together slightly when he concentrated, imagining he was holding his hockey stick. He moved his fingers—not wiggling, but he was able to bend his knuckles slightly. He sent thoughts down to his toes, those same toes that had dug into his skates and sent him sprinting down the ice. He thought he had forced his big toe to brush against the skin of his second toe.

He cast his mind ahead to the next team tryouts. He'd been working on his push and stop motion, the split-second race from one end of the tiny crease to the other, so crucial to perfect as a goaltender. Mr. Leah had encouraged him and Paul to train by dashing down the rink, stopping hard at short intervals, changing the side on which he stopped each time to build his muscles and reflexes. The coach had timed them with a stopwatch to see how many stop/starts they could do in a minute. Dale decided he would use his time in the hospital to maintain his mental agility, so he could get back into action after he recovered. He visualized himself tearing up the ice in instant stops, over and over, getting faster and faster.

He finally dozed off, only to be awakened by the clanking of kitchen carts and food trays a few hours later. He'd been careful to keep his head still since Dr. Barsky took the tube out. His trick had worked, because now he could turn his head with only a little soreness. With his new ability to look left and right, he felt a jolt to see more kids than he could have imagined— at least ten boys on either side of him, all of them in iron lungs, all of them being hand fed by nurses and orderlies hovering over them. The orderly at his side held a spoonful of scrambled eggs, urging him to keep up his progress.

"Do you think I can get out of here soon?" Dale asked between bites. His voice was raspy and thin, and talking was hard work. It took at least twice as long to eat—he could only swallow when he exhaled. If he stopped to talk—also when he exhaled—it took even longer.

"No promises," Morley replied, adding a drop of ketchup to the eggs. "I've seen a lot of kids walk out of here—no braces, no surgery—and they're fine. No promises, but we'll hope for the best. Here, have another bite."

Dale chewed, waiting for the machine to force him to exhale so he could swallow safely. "Have you worked here for a long time?"

"Only a few months," Morley said, offering him a spoonful of porridge. "With luck, the new vaccine they're giving little kids will mean fewer people get polio. Wouldn't that be something? Oops, sorry," he laughed. He took the edge of the spoon and scraped a dollop of porridge he'd dropped on Dale's cheek.

"It sure would be." Dale's thoughts flashed to Brent. He was certain his dad would have come to his senses about the right thing to do. He knew his dad wanted the best for Brent. Morley fed Dale a few more bites, wiped his mouth, and moved on to the next patient.

Mostly, Dale wanted to see his father and show him

that he could move again. He could hardly wait for the afternoon. A voice interrupted his thoughts.

"I hear you're getting sprung out of there soon."

"Huh?" Dale turned his head to the right to see a boy in a wheelchair. A shock of black hair dangled down his forehead. His blue hospital bathrobe hung loosely on his tall, lanky frame, and his matching pajamas were open at the throat. His right arm was secured in front of him in a white cotton sling.

"Yeah," the boy said. He stared directly at Dale with penetrating blue eyes. "I hear you passed the test." Behind him, Charlene rolled up in her own chair. Today, she wore her hair down, held back by a violet hair band.

"This is George," Charlene said from her chair. "He's seen a lot of kids come and go, so he thinks he can diagnose how you'll do."

"Keeps me busy," George said over his shoulder to Charlene. Turning back to Dale, he said, "You play hockey? Which team?"

Dale perked up at the mention of hockey. "I'm a goalie—West Kildonan Bisons," he said. "You play?"

"Pfft," George blew from his lips. "You mean 'played,'" he said. "I *played* left wing for the Carmen Beavers."

He used his left arm to pick up his right hand, which fell limp in the sling, then pointed to his right leg. Mindful of his throat, Dale angled his head a bit more to peer downward. George lifted his pajama leg to reveal the calf muscles gnarled around the bone, while his foot contorted inward.

"Gruesome, isn't it?" George said, a mocking tone in his voice. "I don't think I'll be slapping the puck in the net anytime soon. Likely you won't be stopping any, either."

"Quiet, George," Charlene hissed, leaning toward him. "You have no idea how he'll recover. Stop being so negative."

George tossed his head, the hair hanging down, landing over his eyes. "Listen to her," he said. "She'll get married and have someone take care of her, but I'm useless for absolutely anything."

"Stop feeling sorry for yourself," Charlene said, moving her chair in beside George's. "No one's going to save me, and I don't intend to do nothing all my life. Don't listen to him, Dale. I want to be a nurse, and I'm going to do it."

George spun his left wheel, so his chair zipped around to face Charlene.

"I'm not sorry for myself. It's true, though. That operation they want me to have on my leg won't make me able to skate, and I'll never be able to take over my dad's farm. What will I be able to do, Charlene—dust my old trophies?" He whipped his chair back so that he faced Dale.

"Get yourself into one of these chariots," he said, taking in a breath, his rage suddenly evaporating. He patted the armrests on his wheelchair. "We race when the nurses aren't watching. Gotta have some fun." He reached into the pocket of his housecoat and pulled out a box of Bridge Mixture chocolates. He shook one out and offered one each to Dale and Charlene. "My parents bring them," he said, "so I share them around. See ya later." He rolled himself away.

"Jeez," Dale said to Charlene. She popped his treat into his mouth, advising him to tuck it inside his cheek so the chocolate would take a long time to dissolve. His joy over his personal achievements had vanished with George's foul temper. "Is he always like this?

"He's notorious for being moody," Charlene said, brushing her hair back over her shoulder. "He has bad days, and he's worried about the operation they want to do on his leg. But he doesn't mean it," she said. "He really is a nice guy. My friend Karen is head over heels in love with him. She thinks he's dreamy." A smile lit up her face, as her eyes followed George's path down the ward. Dale's heart flipped. She looked back at him. "The wheelchair races really are fun, you know. You'll see."

"Oh, I don't know," Dale said, furrowing his brow. He experienced a twinge of dismay that Charlene hadn't understood his goal. "I might get out of here soon ..."

Charlene shook her head. "You're here for a while, Dale," she said. "Get used to it."

"I've got to train for the start of hockey in the fall," he explained. She clearly didn't understand. "Do you like hockey?" he asked, hopeful for a little conversation.

"Hockey ... uh ... yeah, maybe. I go skating sometimes, but that's all. I don't know," she said, a vague look on her face." Then she smiled. "Listen, you'll go home when you're ready. There's nothing you can do about it. You'll find out." She turned her chair around. "My mother and father are coming this afternoon. I have to put on real clothes. See you later." She rolled off.

A nurse carrying a metal basin and a washcloth appeared beside Dale. "Visiting hours start at two," she said. "I've got a lot to do, so let's get you ready." Setting the bowl down on the table beside his iron lung, she squeezed water out of the washcloth and, without asking permission, began scrubbing his face and hair.

His father looked uncomfortable, standing beside the iron lung, holding the rim of his gray fedora in both hands and circling it round and round with his fingers. His spring coat was unbuttoned to reveal his navy blue checked sport jacket and white shirt, open at the collar.

"Where have you been?" Dale asked.

Dad raised a questioning eyebrow. "I've been checking up on you, Dale. I called the doctor every day when I got home from work. But I have to take care of Brent, don't I?" he said. "It's time to get the yardwork started, you know—I have to take advantage of the weather, and I have to work..." He gave Dale an awkward smile. "But they're taking care of you here, aren't they? Are you listening to the doctors?"

"What are you talking about?" Dale asked, his anger flaring. He knew his dad was unhappy. They'd been annoyed with each other since his mom had died, but Dale was his son, and his father had no right to abandon him. He gulped for air. "I'm sick, Dad. Really sick."

"I know," Dad said, looking away. He turned his fedora some more. "That's why I'm here—to see how you're doing."

"Where's Brent?"

"With Grandma," his father said.

"Why doesn't she come?"

"She's ... she's not sure ..." his dad's voice trailed off as he looked away. Dale turned to see what his father saw—long, cream-colored monsters, perched on wheels with the heads of children stuck on the ends like knobs. The large pressure gauges on top reminded him of equipment he'd seen on steam engines. He was inside one, too.

The boys were all ages. Some were alone, pretending not to notice that others had visitors. Some parents bent their heads sideways to attempt to be on an equal footing with their children. A few parents had pulled the cotton dividers around their little group to create a private space for their visit. There was some laughter and a lot of silence.

"When can I go home?" Dale asked.

"Home? I ..." his father struggled. "I don't know,

Dale. You're ... paralyzed!" he blurted out. "I can't take care of you!"

Dale began to cry.

"Stop it," Dad commanded quietly, his eyes searching the ward surreptitiously to see if anyone was watching. His face was red, and he turned his hat in his fingers even faster. "Don't blame me. How am I supposed to help you? You can't walk."

Dale shifted his head on his pillow. Inside the iron lung, his hand moved and he flexed his foot.

"I've got to go," Dad said.

"You're going? But you—"

"It's a long ride. I had to take the streetcar and the bus to get here."

"What?" Dale wished he could stand up and look directly at his father. "Does Mr. Leah know I'm here? Tell him I'll be back in time for tryouts," he said from his machine. "I'll be okay soon. Tell him I'm practicing."

His father put his fedora on his head, pulled at the brim, then rubbed his jaw. "Hockey?" He motioned his hand along the iron lung. "Dale, you're not playing hockey anymore. I told you before this happened, and now—good grief, son," he said, clearly becoming agitated, "you're paralyzed. There's no more hockey."

He pulled at the hat brim again, and looked down the row of children trapped in their iron prisons. "I'll see you soon," he said, and tapped the top of his son's machine. Hesitating for a moment, he said, "Goodbye," turned around and walked away, his head bent forward.

"Wait, Dad." Dale tried calling out, but his voice was still too weak to carry any distance. "Tell me more about Brent!"

CHAPTER 6

"Stop, you're killing me!" Dale screamed.

"Ach, Dale, don't be such a baby," Mrs. Stewart laughed. The physiotherapist held the wool blankets taut around Dale's calves, despite his efforts to wiggle out backward. "Hold still," she commanded, working her fingers through the wool and massaging Dale's leg muscles. The pressure on his rigid muscles was intense. "Do you want to get back on the ice, young man, or not? Remember ..." she lifted her eyes to the sign on the wall: *No pain, no gain!*

Mrs. Stewart's slogan was painted on a board and hung like a threat above the exercise tables, italicized to show motion—action! There were others—one with a drawing of a tortoise crossing the finish line, while a hare struggled to catch up—*Slow and steady wins the race*, it reminded the patients. Another drawing of a ladder showed a bottom rung inscribed with the words

I can't do it, followed by the rung above, *I might try, but just once*, then *I'm trying, but it hurts*, and at the top, *I did it!* The slogans mocked him and all the other kids fighting their bodies, fighting the people who fought with their bodies. He wanted to rip them off the wall of the room, which he thought of as a giant torture chamber.

He gritted his teeth. He regretted his outburst, but he'd been unable to hold back. He also wished Mrs. Stewart hadn't been told he played hockey. Maybe she would be less brutal with him if he merely wanted to learn to walk again. At least, she would stop laughing openly at him.

"This will get you started," Mrs. Stewart said. She removed the old wrappings as the assistant arrived beside his padded exercise table with a pot of near-boiling water. "Sit back now and rest."

He cringed at Mrs. Stewart's instructions. How could he rest with his skin flaming and itching under wet wool blankets? Using large tongs, the assistant moved long strips of old, heavy wool blankets into a wringer, squeezing out the excess water. But there was plenty of heat left in the wool. It scalded his skin as they quickly bound him up, then encased the blankets in towels to keep the warmth in longer. The wool reeked of sheep, while the heat and prickliness were more than most kids could bear—shrieks of "No!" and "Take it off!" regularly emanated from the physiotherapy room.

No objections or insults seemed to phase Mrs. Stewart.

"It's like she was born to do this," Charlene said. She lay on a table not far from Dale, her legs also swathed in hot wool. "Her vocation, as they say," she laughed, wriggling her fingers underneath the itchy material to scratch.

Mrs. Stewart reprimanded Charlene with a firm swat. "Ach, lassie, he's making good progress," she said in her Scottish burr. "Out of there!" She moved Charlene's hand away and pulled the wool tighter around her legs.

"She's heartless!" Charlene exclaimed across the tables to Dale. "Aren't you, Mrs. Stewart?" She'd been in the hospital so long that she and Mrs. Stewart knew each other well.

"Do you want to walk again?" Mrs. Stewart asked Charlene, not waiting for an answer. "It's not a piece of cake; it's a hard, hard task. And can you see how hard this is for me?" she complained. "Look how I'm working to get you up and on your feet. And you will walk, lass.

In the two years since I came to Winnipeg, I've made sure my patients do their best." She wagged her finger at both of them. "You'll be out of that chair sooner rather than later, if I have anything to do with it."

"Is that why you left Scotland?" Charlene joked. "To torment kids in Winnipeg?"

"Ach." Mrs. Stewart swatted Charlene again, but with laughing eyes. "You kids are sassy, but I'm used to it. I nursed wounded soldiers in the war, so I've heard lots of complaining and kidding." She tugged at the wool strips on Dale's legs, checking for tightness.

"You did?" Charlene asked. "Are you a nurse, too? Where were you?"

"Oh, yes, I'm a fully qualified nurse, but I prefer to work in therapy," she said. "I like to see the progress you kids make. I worked as a nurse in country hospitals in England. They were set up away from large cities, where the Germans were bombing," she said.

"Oh." Charlene perked up. "What was it like?"

Mrs. Stewart slowed her tugging. "Ach, well," she said softly. "I have plenty of stories, but they aren't all happy. I did what I could to help out, though. We can talk about it sometime."

"I want to be a nurse," Charlene declared.

"Ah, then for sure, we'll have a wee chat," Mrs. Stewart said, smiling.

"Why did you come to Winnipeg?" Dale asked. He propped himself up on his elbows.

"Well, that's another story," Mrs. Stewart said. "I was born in Scotland, but when I married, we lived in England, where my husband is from. But the whole country needed rebuilding after all the bombing in the war, and finally we decided to rebuild our own lives in Canada. England has gloomy weather, and we were told Winnipeg had a lot of sunny days, and we thought, 'Why not?' Our daughter loves it here, so this is our home now."

She shook her head. "Back to business, now. Leave those bindings alone for twenty minutes. I have to work with those bairns over there." She pointed to kids at the other end of the room, waiting by a set of exercise bars. "I'll be back soon."

"Bears?" Dale asked.

"Bairns," Mrs. Stewart called out, looking back as she walked away. "That's Gaelic for 'children,' Dale. But I could tame a bear, if I wanted to," she winked.

Charlene stifled a laugh behind her hand.

It did feel like he was being tortured, Dale thought, but being close to Charlene gave him more to think about than his pain. She told him all about the hospital ward, the nurses who were nice and those who were crochety, the kids who had come and gone, the kids who had come and stayed.

"It's a little town," she told him. "Lots of gossip, too!" She had a hearty laugh.

"Are you ever going home?" Dale asked her. "Do you live in the city?"

Charlene's smile twisted as she answered. "Sure I do. Not that far away," she said, motioning with her head. "On Hector Avenue, but the doctors don't think I should go home." She looked away.

"Why not?"

"Ah," she said, pausing for a moment, her smile becoming a frown. "They don't think I can live there if I'm still in a wheelchair. We don't have indoor plumbing, so it will be hard to use an outhouse, and we have to haul water, so I can't turn on a tap if I want some. The house is small, too. I have three sisters, and there isn't a lot of room." She turned to look at him. "That's why I want to get strong enough to walk on crutches. I want to go home."

"You don't have plumbing or running water—and you live in Winnipeg?" Dale asked. "I've never heard of that." He thought of his family's house on Smithfield Avenue. It wasn't fancy, but it had all the modern services he expected a city should provide. Outhouses were on farms, or at cabins on a lake or in the woods. "How come?"

"How do I know?" Charlene said. "That's where we live. The streets a few blocks away have everything, but Rooster Town doesn't have anything." She shrugged. "My parents say it's because we're half-breeds. We don't count."

This was all new to Dale. "Sorry," he said. "I don't get any of that. What's Rooster Town?"

"It's where I live," Charlene said, wrinkling her brow at his ignorance. "None of our houses have running water or plumbing. The streets aren't paved, either, so the nurses and doctors think I won't be able to move around."

"Your streets aren't paved?"

"Nope, they're mud." She paused and her voice became almost angry. "That's why they want my parents to leave me here—or send me to a foster home."

"Why doesn't your family move?"

"But that's where we live!" she said quickly, then crunched her cheek. "And so do some of my relatives. Anyway, you don't get it. It's not easy to move," she said. "My dad and my uncle work for the city, but landlords don't care if they have jobs. My uncle wanted to move, so my dad went to see a few houses with him. But they took a look at them," she lifted her hand to show her brown skin, "and all of a sudden, they said the house had been rented, that it wasn't available anymore, but then the ad was still in the newspaper the next day. It happened over and over."

"Why?"

She scoffed, "Because we're Métis, dummy. Half-Indian, half-French. No one really likes us. Anyway," she said again, looking up at the ceiling, "at least here, no one refuses to touch me. Well, mostly. A few people don't like me because of my skin."

Dale wanted more than anything to hold Charlene's slender brown hand. "What? Because you have polio?"

"No, not that. You're only contagious for a week or two when you get it, and my parents brought me here as soon as I got sick. No, I'm talking about what happens at school." She looked past Dale at the wall. "A few kids at school won't touch us if we're playing a game, or they won't sit near us. Their parents tell them we're dirty because our skin is brown—the kids admitted it. Only a few, but it's so mean." She grimaced and looked back at him. "Some of the nurses think that, too. I can tell. Miss Clements can hardly hide it. If I've touched anything, she treats it like it's contaminated." She shifted her eyes to the ceiling. "I mean, it's better here, but I miss my family. My parents come visit, but my sisters can't—kids under sixteen years old can't come visit, and they're all younger than I am."

Dale couldn't say anything. He'd never heard of anything like this. He thought of the kids in his classes, or on his hockey team—always playing together, sometimes fighting, making fun of each other, but usually making up. He had heard adults make unpleasant comments about "those people," but he'd never actually met anyone he thought they meant. He felt uncomfortable hearing about the kind of treatment Charlene described.

"But I don't care what they say," she said, peeking across the room to see if Mrs. Stewart was watching, then shoving her fingers down the side of the wool strips and scratching furiously. "I'm using the time here to learn about what nurses do. I want to help people the way some of them have helped me. Then I can help my family with money, too."

Again, Dale couldn't speak.

Charlene snorted and broke into a big grin. "Maybe I'll be another Miss Clements," she hiss-whispered, and waved her hands in a commanding way. "Do it yourself! I'm not your servant. Or maybe I'll be like Mrs. Stewart. 'Ach, lassie,'" she said, doing a terrible job of mimicking a Scottish accent.

She and Dale both broke into peals of laughter. He liked her even more. He gasped as he laughed; he could breathe independently now, but his lungs weren't quite ready for bouts of hysteria.

"Wha's this?" Mrs. Stewart said, suddenly at Dale's side. "Enough jokes, dearie."

Charlene blushed but played dumb, and pretended not to watch Mrs. Stewart working with him.

Mrs. Stewart peeled away the now-cool strips of wool to reveal Dale's pink, tender limbs. She squeezed a few drops of baby oil on her hands and greased them liberally. "Let's go, lad," she said, and began massaging Dale's legs, pulling and stretching his muscles against their will, yet lightening her touch when he grimaced in pain. Still, she put all her effort into the kneading and pummeling of his calves, thighs, his back, biceps, and hands. By the time she was done, he felt like a piece of raw meat. Through it all, Dale kept thinking about what Charlene had told him.

"It's time to try walking, young man. You're ready," Mrs. Stewart announced.

Dale couldn't believe what he was hearing. It had been weeks since he'd walked on his own. Hockey had been in his thoughts, but at the same time, being lifted and transferred had become his reality. A shiver of excitement and fear zipped through him.

In the next moment, Mrs. Stewart plunked him in his wheelchair, and maneuvered it in front of two raised parallel wooden bars. They stood on a gray mat, set there to cushion the fall of the many patients who collapsed when their arms gave way. A full-length mirror hung on the opposite wall, so the patient could see his or her efforts, and supposedly be inspired by them. Dale and the other kids saw the mirror as a reflection of their weaknesses, of skills they'd lost. Some kids wouldn't look.

"Pull yourself up, Dale," Mrs. Stewart said. He reached forward and hauled himself up, only then realizing how weak his arms had become. It was hard. When he glanced in the mirror, he winced—what a wounded warrior he was, a caricature of a hockey star. He looked away.

"Never you mind about that," Mrs. Stewart said, reading his mind. "Wait a few days and you'll see a different Dale. Now, put your right hand forward and try to pull your right leg with it." Her eyes were on his hands and legs. She held her hands wide, ready to catch him.

"Good job, all right. Now the left hand," she instructed. "Lift your left foot as well."

Dale held his breath and willed his legs to move. Pain sliced through his shoulders and arms as they bore his weight. His legs twitched, as the nerves in his muscles came alive, and sent stabbing jolts through them when he tried to drag them. But ever so slowly, they obeyed his command. He broke out in a sweat.

Maybe those annoying signs on the wall were right. If he worked hard, he would be ready for hockey tryouts in the fall, Dale thought. He was a tortoise right now, but he would cross the finish line. He looked up to see himself in the mirror. The boy who stared back smiled at him.

"Good lad!" Mrs. Stewart declared, then drew him back into the wheelchair. "Tha's enough for today. You're on the way, young man. You're on the way." She nodded in satisfaction.

"Good job, Dale," Charlene said. Her tone was upbeat but forlorn. Her legs dangled over the edge of her table. Dale could see her calf muscles were scrawny from lack of use. She'd been in a wheelchair for a long time, and they needed building up.

"You'll get there," he told her. She gave him her magic smile again.

An orderly handed out packages of Dubble Bubble gum to all the kids, as a reward for a job well done, then turned the radio on loud, tuning it to the regular episode of *Gunsmoke*. Marshall Matt Dillon used his wits to keep gunslingers and cattle rustlers in line in the Old West. It was a brief moment of distraction. Dale wondered if there had been any polio epidemics threatening the cowboys in Dodge City.

He slowly unwrapped his prize and began to chew the sticky gum, along with all the other kids, blowing bubbles to exercise their jaws and cheek muscles. Amid the popping noises and laughter from faces decorated with burst bubbles, he wondered how he would feel if people refused to touch him or sit next to him in school.

CHAPTER 7

Despite loathing the prospect of daily physiotherapy, Dale was now able to flex his toes, thanks to Mrs. Stewart's instructions to pick up marbles with them. He also diligently followed her directives to avoid developing "dropfoot." Some kids whose legs were permanently paralyzed lost muscle tone in their feet; their toes pointed uselessly and permanently downward. Every night, he pushed his feet against the plywood board installed at the bottom of his bed, bending them at the toe and the arch to strengthen them. The pain ricocheting up and down his ankles and calves made him wince, but he feared he would never skate again unless he persevered. As he practiced, he wondered if Paul was working on his skills, too. Dale didn't care what his father commanded— he knew he would play hockey again. He and his dad had different ideas of success, he decided. Dale had lived and breathed hockey for too long to give it up.

But his father hadn't come back since his one and only visit nearly two weeks earlier, although Dr. Barsky assured him he called regularly to check on his condition. Dale wasn't sure if he was angry at him or relieved. He hoped his dad was taking good care of Brent, even though he expected most of his time would be spent working silently on chores around the house, rather than playing with his son.

Without telling Mrs. Stewart, Dale massaged his legs and arms himself, after the ward lights were turned off every night. His hands hurt a lot as he did it, because he couldn't bend his fingers, but he thought his efforts might be helping both his legs and his hands. If anything, he hoped any progress could bring an end to the hated hot wool wrappings.

"Tha's it, you're done," Mrs. Stewart announced the next day, after an hour's prodding and walking a few steps again. The treatments called for gradual advances. After he'd graduated from the iron lung, he'd transferred to a rocking bed for a few hours every day, to relieve the stress on his lungs. He hadn't realized how exhausting the act of breathing could be!

"Teeter-totter time," Morley said, as he strapped

Dale to the rocking bed and switched it on. Up and down, up and down, Dale's head and feet traded places every five seconds, his guts being squeezed against his diaphragm to push the air out when his head went down, then sliding back into place so he could fill his lungs again when his head went up. Squeeze, slosh, squeeze, slosh.

The blood rushed to his head when he tilted downward, making him dizzy and nauseous, until he got used to it. But the rocking motion helped inch him along the road to breathing normally, so he didn't complain. Four other kids rocked along with him in the large, bright sunporch overlooking the front of the hospital. Fresh air blew in through the big screens—it was almost as good as being outside. Morley had set all the beds to move at the same pace, so at least the kids could talk while they watched the world outdoors, the buds growing on the trees, the grass turning green, the clouds rolling past. "Don't go anywhere without me," he joked as he left them.

"He's a real card, isn't he? A first-rate comedian," Lindsay commented wryly from the rocking bed beside Dale's, gulping his air to breathe, delivering his remarks as he exhaled. "How do you like riding this pony?" he said, tapping the rocking bed.

"It seems to help," Dale said. "Dr. Barsky says I'll only need to use it for another week or so. How long have you used it?"

"Me?" Lindsay snorted. "I'm a champion rocker. I've been here for two years, and I use it every day. The hospital is going to be my permanent address, so you can call me the Rocker King of King George."

Dale was taken aback. "What do you mean? Why can't you ever go home? Isn't your breathing getting better at all?"

"If 'frog breathing' is getting better."

Dale watched Lindsay closely, and realized that he had to plan every breath, lifting his shoulders and throwing his head up to straighten his windpipe, pulling the air into his lungs, then lowering his chin to expel it.

"I can only do this for a few hours on my own, and those chest respirators they wrap me in aren't comfortable for very long," Lindsay said. "And my family lives way out in the sticks. My mom and dad run a sheep farm outside of Langruth. It's a nice place if you're a waterbird, but you can't have an iron lung and a rocking bed out there. I can't breathe without the lung at night or the bed during the day. Too dangerous, they say. We get electrical failures all the time, and the neighbors aren't close. The doctor is miles away, too. No more listening to the hooting of loons for me. Actually," he said, a tinge of sadness in his voice, "I liked hearing that sound in the mornings." He gulped.

"What about your family?"

"What about them? They'll keep going. I've got two little brothers and two little sisters that keep my parents busy. They'll forget about their big brother. I haven't even met one of my brothers, so he'll think I'm a long-lost relative." He snorted as he expelled his breath.

"Why don't you know him?" Dale felt dizzy at this unhappy story.

"My mother got pregnant after I got sick. She stayed away until the baby was born, and then for a long time after. Anyway, they don't have much. They can't afford the cost of gas for the truck that often, and if they brought the kids, they'd all have to stay overnight at a motel. It's too complicated and expensive. So—I've never met my baby brother. My mom says he looks like me, too." He pinched his lips together as he rocked up and down. "He's over a year old now. He's probably chasing the sheep through the pasture already." His head disappeared and bobbed back up.

Dale didn't know what to say.

"Hey, you think that half-breed's cute, eh?" Lindsay said.

Dale jerked to attention. "Huh?"

"Charlene—she's a half-breed. Can't you tell?" Lindsay jibed. "Why would you be interested in someone with Indian in her?"

Dale stayed silent, the hum of the rocking bed filling the space, while he processed the meaning of Lindsay's remarks. Lindsay turned his head toward Dale, a small smile on his lips. Dale avoided his gaze. He felt like he'd been punched in the gut. Lindsay was the kind of person Charlene talked about.

His unease was broken by a cheery voice announcing herself. "Here I am!"

A rocking bed was a strange place to do schoolwork, but a teacher had shown up a few days earlier, and declared she would help Dale keep up with his classwork. Mrs. Morris didn't pay any attention to Dale's head disappearing and reappearing several times a minute. They'd worked on math exercises already, and she'd called Dale's school to ask for other assignments. Pulling up a chair, she crossed her legs, swung her wavy blonde hair behind her ear, and opened a textbook on her lap to reveal a letter between the pages.

Mrs. Morris took a handwritten paper out of the envelope. "Aha, here's your science assignment, Dale," she said, her bright red lipstick stretching into a grin. "Your teacher says you're doing well enough in math that you'll be able to keep going in September, and he'll forgive you writing a final English exam, if you do a good job on the essay you were talking about. So, you will pass to Grade 9, okay?" She smiled and read the notes silently. "Which topic had you chosen?"

"Uh ..." His brain felt like mush. He'd worried about missing his schoolwork, fearful that he'd have to repeat Grade 8 because of all the time he'd missed. Mrs. Morris's announcement gave him a sense of relief, except now he had to concentrate to make sure he fulfilled his teacher's expectation. But the act of thinking was harder than he'd expected. It seemed so long ago that he'd been in school. "Gregor Mendel and his discovery of heredity," he remembered. "He figured out family traits using pea pods."

"Right," Mrs. Morris said, knocking her pen on her books. She studied the letter. "Gregor Mendel ..." she hesitated.

"My dad could go to the library for me. He'll bring the books so I can do the research." Maybe that would force him to come visit, Dale thought.

"No, he can't," Lindsay chimed in. "Not unless you don't mind the hospital burning them after you're done."

"What? Why in the world would they want to burn a book? A library book, too." He didn't trust Lindsay at all now.

"Don't you know?" Lindsay said, his body swaying up and down as the engine in the bed hummed. He gulped air between phrases. "Because everyone on the outside thinks we're still infectious. Even though the hospital knows better, they don't let you take anything out of here." He sniffed. "We're lepers. Even my parents are afraid of me."

Mrs. Morris intervened. "I saw you with your parents last summer, Lindsay. They were so happy to see you. I know your mom filled you in about everything that was going on at the farm."

Lindsay ignored her. He turned to Dale. "Do you

know, they bring a separate set of clothes to change into when they leave. I've watched them from the window here. They arrive with a bag, which I guess they leave downstairs, and they're carrying the bag but wearing different clothes to go home." He huffed some air through his nose. "They probably wish I'd died. It would be a lot easier on everybody, including me." Lindsay's voice was flat. "I know I'd prefer it, instead of spending my life watching people leave."

He huffed again. "That's why, when you go home, the hospital will burn anything you have. You'll only have the clothes you leave with, all washed clean." He rocked up and down, up and down. "So—don't ask your dad to get books from the library, Dale. He won't be able to return them."

Lindsay's remarks about Charlene had repelled Dale. Yet he felt sympathy for him, too, considering his plight. As soon as he'd started feeling better, Dale had thought less about dying, but Lindsay was stuck in the same place, never going anywhere.

What if Dale's fate were the same as Lindsay's? What if all the practicing in his mind and thinking about hockey was for nothing? He thought about Paul and all the opportunities that were opening up for him. Dark thoughts returned.

He wished his father would come, so he could ask his opinion about what Lindsay was implying, about who he could like.

A strained silence hung in the air. Mrs. Morris cleared her throat and adopted her teacher voice again. "Let's talk about your assignment, Dale," she said, as his rocking bed tilted up and down. "Your topic is fine, but—well, take a look around you." She swept her hand toward all the kids on the rocking beds, and then toward the sheet of paper. "One of the questions on this list is about vaccinations, and they've got a new vaccine for polio. Why don't you write about vaccines?"

"Vaccines?" he said. "But there aren't any books about the polio vaccine yet, are there?"

"Maybe not, but there is a lot of information about other diseases. Smallpox killed millions of people over the centuries. Then they developed a vaccine. Why don't you write about how it was discovered and what happened because of it? We have a set of encyclopedias in the hospital library. The same ideas apply to polio."

Dale looked out onto the park that surrounded the

hospital. The sun shone and the landscape was turning greener every day, but he felt dull inside. Mrs. Morris tapped his hand.

"Dale," she said firmly. "I can't help you with your polio, but I can get you through this by keeping your schoolwork up. I'll go downstairs and get what you need from the library," she said, packing up her papers and books. "I'll see you tomorrow, both of you," she said, pointing to Lindsay as well. "Remember, chin up!" She brushed her hand under her chin and lifted her head.

"Do you have kids at home, Mrs. Morris?" Lindsay had been paying attention the whole time.

"Yes, I do," the teacher replied, her blue eyes lighting up. "I have two sons, nine and twelve years old. Now, I have to work with some of the other children. See you soon," she said, and gave them both a big smile as she left.

"I wonder if she changes her clothes before she goes home," Lindsay smirked.

CHAPTER 8

He slammed shut the book that Mrs. Morris had brought him. He'd read the same line over and over, thinking about Charlene. Why shouldn't he like her? Did she know he liked her? Did she like him? How could he pretend not to like her? He didn't want to be subjected to Lindsay's sneering comments. Did other people think that way? Why couldn't he stand up to Lindsay?

He'd written his thoughts down on paper that was supposed to be used for his essay. His arms were stronger, but his fingers still didn't bend properly. Clasping the pen was an exercise in itself. His childish writing embarrassed him, the letters straying everywhere. It took him a long time to get it all down, but he'd hoped he could come to a conclusion by writing it out. In the end, he was no further ahead. His mother's face loomed at him as he wrote, some comments she had once made echoing in his mind, making him worry more.

They used to talk about things in the kitchen, while she washed the dishes after supper, and he dried them. Usually, they were enjoyable chats, but a feeling of dread came over him when he remembered a few conversations they'd had. She'd told him stories about relatives or neighbors who had dated someone from a different religion.

"His parents were against it," she said, scrubbing at a piece of food stuck inside a pot, recalling a cousin who'd become engaged to a woman of a different religion. "They wouldn't accept her, and finally the couple broke up."

"What happened to him?" Dale asked, engrossed. He swirled the towel over a plate for the fourth time.

"Eventually, he married someone who was the same religion," she said, rinsing the pot. "As he should have. You marry someone just like you. It works out best that way. One of my schoolmates married out of her religion, and her parents disowned her—told her she was dead to them, wouldn't talk about her or meet their grandchildren."

"What? Really?"

"What did she expect?" Mom said, putting the pot in the drainer and shaking her head. "She should have stuck with her own. Otherwise, where do you belong?

Where do your kids belong?" She pulled the stopper from the drain, and the water swooshed toward the center of the sink.

Dale's heart hurt whenever he thought about his mother, which was many times a day. She and his dad were from the same religion, but she hadn't said anything about color. What would she say, even if two people were the same religion?

Since his mother died, Dale and his dad had quarreled, first over little things. His dad was always irritable. Then came Dad's decision that Dale had to withdraw from hockey, which Dale couldn't forgive. He thought more and more about how sweet and kind his mother had been. But would she disown him if he fell in love with someone like Charlene?

It's no fun having Lindsay embarrass me, and I have to see him every day. He's so good at being mean, and he likes it.

Karen appeared suddenly beside his bed, startling him. He folded the paper quickly and tucked it into the book.

"Here comes your dream girl," she said, giggling.

She pointed with her crutch to show him that Charlene was on her way.

"What are you talking about?" Dale whispered, his face folding into a frown.

"Did you think you could keep it a secret?" Karen laugh-whispered. "You melt whenever you're near her. Everyone knows it." She cupped her hand at the side of her face and said, "She likes you, too," then covered her mouth to hide a huge grin.

"Be quiet," Dale hissed. "Be quiet." His worry increased. Did she really like him?

Braces on Karen's legs and arms kept them straight. They were secured around clunky black tie-up shoes with built-up heels—"old lady's shoes," the kids called them. Crutches made her appear like a wobbly robot. She was walking independently for the first time, grasping the handles, but she still tottered. Every step was taken with care.

Dale's breathing had stabilized, with shorter and fewer stints on the rocker bed. He could flex his feet and wiggle his toes and fingers, but Mrs. Stewart said she wouldn't trust him to walk on his own yet. Neither would he.

Dale wondered when his dad would be coming

back; he wanted to show off what he could do, to show his father recovery was possible nearly three weeks in, even if it wasn't as quick as he wanted. And he had so many questions to ask—he needed his dad.

If his mother were still alive, he'd ask her—maybe.

A squealing noise brought him back to the present. "Look at you!" Charlene hooted at Karen as she wheeled up, thumping her armrests. Her laugh echoed, and Dale liked her even more. "You'll be a fashion model walking down a runway soon!" Charlene cooed.

Karen exploded in giggles. "A runway of wobblers, maybe. That would be a sight—crutches, braces, wheel-chairs!" She closed her eyes, arched her neck back, and swished her long brown hair across the shoulders of her pink chenille bathrobe.

"In the latest dressing gown fashions! George will be gaga over you," Charlene said. Karen blushed, then the two girls caught each other's eyes.

"Hey!" they both cried at the same time, and before Dale knew it, the girls were planning a fashion show.

"I'll be the commentator," Karen told Charlene. "I'll announce each of the models and describe the latest in bedwear!"

"We can play records," Charlene replied, bubbling with excitement. "I've got 'Hey There!'—we can sing along, the same way Rosemary Clooney sings it on the radio—all dreamy-like about stars in our eyes. Do you think we can convince some boys to get haircuts so they can sing with The Crewcuts, 'Hello, Hello Again!'" she crooned. "I love that song."

They broke into a fit of laughter again, while Dale endured their gabbing. One of the boys on the ward called out, "Stop that screeching!" which made them sing louder and laugh more.

Dale had hoped to impress Charlene with what he was reading. More than a thousand years ago in China, Africa, and Turkey, people had figured out how to build immunity to smallpox. They scratched their skin open and touched it with a drop of pus from the blister of another person who had a mild form of the disease. They called it "variolation." In 1796, a British doctor, Edward Jenner, perfected the process of vaccination, using material from cowpox. But the information that caught his interest was something he'd never heard of before. There had been opposition to the smallpox vaccine, ranging from the notion that vaccines were "unchristian," to being a violation of an individual's freedom, when the vaccines were declared compulsory in the nineteenth century, to keep the disease from spreading and killing people. He thought he might include this in his essay. His hands were getting stronger, and maybe writing a whole essay would take him that much closer to holding a hockey stick.

What did a vaccine have to do with religion, and why would anyone want to risk getting sick and possibly dying, he wondered? And why should anyone be allowed to infect other people? He would have done anything not to have polio.

But Charlene didn't seem to notice him today. He almost felt relieved—he didn't know if he should let his feelings toward her rule his fears, or let his fears rule his feelings.

George rolled up in his wheelchair, a newspaper on his lap. His arm still lay limp in the sling, and his feet drooped from lack of use. Still, despite pushing his chair with only one arm, he drove straight. "I was pretty good at stick-handling," he had told Dale, winking and showing the confidence he must have had as a hockey player. "I use the same skills to direct the wheels."

Karen gushed and stammered their plan to him while Charlene laughed at her friend's nervousness.

George didn't seem to notice. "You two are nuts," he pronounced, when he learned he was expected to be a male model in the fashion show, and protested, "I'm not getting a crewcut," as Charlene and Karen wheeled and teetered away to the girls' ward, looking to enlist others they were already labeling "willing wobblers."

Dale imagined George's long black locks being sheared off into a buzzcut, just to sing a song.

George tossed the newspaper onto Dale's bed. "Baseball season's started. I'm rooting for the Yankees."

"I thought you were a hockey fan," Dale said. He reached over and dragged the newspaper to be able to see it.

"All sports, all the time," George said.

"My hockey coach writes for the sports section," Dale said, and pointed out Vince Leah's name on the masthead of the sports section. "He knows everything about any sport—baseball, hockey, you name it. You probably read his articles nearly every day."

"Hmph ... the way things are going, reading is all I'll be able to do," George said. He drew his fingers back through the messy cowlick that drooped over his eyes. It fell back immediately.

"You never know," Dale said.

George gave him a "let's not pretend" look.

"Sorry," Dale said. "Honest. I really am." He paused, then asked, "How did you get sick?"

George huffed and smiled, "Well, if you ask the quack who was our family doctor, I was faking it. He made fun of my mother for keeping me home from school, when I couldn't get out of bed that morning. He didn't even examine me—said I probably forgot to do my homework and didn't want to go to school. He recommended a good dose of castor oil to ease the pain in my stomach, which he also thought I was faking. My mom told him off, real good." He gazed down the aisle. "My dad was working at another farm that day. She called over and they hauled me into the car and drove like madmen all the way to the city."

He looked at Dale. "I've been here ever since—about eight months now. I don't have to frog breathe anymore, but my lungs aren't strong. I'll never play hockey again. They want to operate and rearrange the muscles in my leg. The doctor says there's an outside chance I might be able to walk if they do. Might ... no promises." He thumped his bad leg with his fist. "I don't know what will happen to me."

"Karen doesn't seem to care," Dale said.

"I know." George's voice dropped. "I like her, too, but I don't want to show it, so don't tell her," he warned. "She'll find someone who can walk, and maybe help her out, because she might have to use crutches forever." He sighed. "Ah, well. At least I can keep up with sports. I'd go crazy without the newspaper and the radio."

"Will you be able to go home?"

"Yeah, probably. We live near Altona, and we have everything on the farm. My dad's rebuilding the house in case I have to use the wheelchair. But my older brother and I were going to take over his farm one day. That's what we both wanted to do."

"You won't be able to operate a tractor—"

"—or plant wheat, or cut hay—nope, not with a wheelchair or crutches. I already told my brother I'd keep the books, do the business side of the farm—all the stuff he doesn't like to do, anyway. So, it might work out," he said wistfully, "but it's not what I thought I'd be doing."

The joy Dale felt about his own progress again evaporated into guilt. He looked down the ward to make sure no one was paying attention to their exchange, and to make sure Lindsay was still out at physiotherapy. Lindsay's bed and his iron lung lay empty.

Dale cleared his throat. "George, I have a question." He ran his hand along the edge of the newspaper. "If you'll keep this between you and me."

"Sure," George answered, sliding his strong hand under his weak arm in the sling. "Shoot."

Dale spoke even more quietly. "What do you think of Lindsay?"

George paused, then wagged his head slightly. "Him? He's okay, I guess. Says stupid things once in a while, but who doesn't?" He shrugged.

"He made fun of me because I like Charlene. He called her a half-breed." The words sounded ugly coming from his mouth.

George raised his eyebrows. "Yeah, my dad said something about her, too, that I shouldn't get any ideas." He paused, angling his wheels to the left, then back to the center again. He took his good hand out of the sling and waved a finger to imitate his mother.

"My mom says, 'You have to marry one of your own,' so I guess she thinks the same way, which means I can only choose a white Anglican. Maybe a white Anglican who also has polio and sits in a wheelchair all day." He laughed, something Dale had rarely seen him do.

"My mother used to say things like that, too," Dale said. "I don't know ..."

"You're fourteen years old. You're not getting married, so who cares what Lindsay thinks?" George said, leaning back in his chair. "Anyway, Charlene's nice—and cute, too." He flicked his cowlick again, and again it fell over his eyes. He laughed. "And I don't know why my mother thinks I can be that picky. I'd have to find an Anglican who wants to date someone who's useless. That narrows the field."

A rattling noise from the doorway caught their attention. An orderly pushing a food cart arrived with the afternoon snack—paper cups filled with vanilla ice cream. "Here you go, boys," he said.

"Dixie cups—my favorite," George said, putting the cup in his lap. He used his teeth to rip the paper on the sleeve that held the little wooden paddle. He let the paddle fall out, then tried to use the index finger of his good hand to pick at the tab on the cover of the ice cream cup, but his fingers couldn't clasp the tiny tab.

Dale turned to ask the orderly to help George, but the man didn't seem to notice the problem. He had set another cup and paddle on Dale's night table and was already off, pushing his cart along.

"What?" George said, when he saw the orderly had left. Just then, Miss Clements walked nearby. "Miss Clements," George called. "Can you help us open our ice cream?"

Miss Clements veered over. "Do you think this is what I'm supposed to be doing?" she snapped, flicking the cover off George's ice cream and tossing it in the small wastebasket. Gruffly, she handed George the paper cup and started to leave.

"What about mine?" Dale said. "The tab is too small for me to pull."

"For goodness sake," she said, turning around. "You boys had better start doing things for yourselves. You're not babies anymore." Without even looking at him, she opened his ice cream and ripped the paper off the paddle. "Here," she said, plunking them down on the night table and walking away.

"Miss Clements," a stern voice called out.

Dale and George both turned to see the nursing supervisor standing in the doorway to the ward. Miss Clements stopped in her tracks.

"I'd like to speak with you, Victoria. Come with me, please. Now," the head nurse said and left the ward. Miss Clements paused, looked to either side, then followed her boss out the door.

"Friendly, isn't she," George commented.

"Born to nurse," Dale mused. "I'd like to hear that conversation." He held the paddle between his thumb and fingers and poked at the ice cream, which had already become soupy. He wondered if there was a way to make Charlene his girlfriend without anyone knowing, and if she would understand why he didn't want to be embarrassed.

CHAPTER 9

"The coast is clear!" Karen whispered loudly. She ducked her head back into the ward. "Quick, before they come back!"

The spectators waited expectantly at the ends of their beds, giggling, pointing at the competitors, and betting on their chances to win. The boys in the iron lungs turned their heads as much as they could toward the door, their eyes shining at the idea of entertainment. The noise of the bellows shoving the air in and out of their bodies was forgotten for a brief time.

It was after lights out, when only the skeleton night staff remained, checking on the different wards in rotation. Before they left the room, the orderlies had pulled down the blinds. But the kids could see the summer sky, reminding them of the long evenings when they had been healthy and played outside, until their mothers nagged them into coming inside.

Tonight's shenanigans were taking place in the boys' ward. Girls who were taking part wheeled or hobbled in, as quietly as they could. A few kids walked around the room, pulling at the cords on the blinds, sending them skyward and letting the light flood back in. They had thirty minutes until the staff came for the first check, so they got busy with their evening's program.

Three kids in wheelchairs lined up for the first heat, and three more waited impatiently for their turn.

Charlene, George, and Peter were ready to go, anticipating the signal, rolling their chairs as if revving their engines.

Karen raised her crutch. "Ready, set, go!" she cried, dropping her crutch to begin the race.

The three kids set off down the aisle, to the hushed cheers and jeers of the spectators. "Go!" "Oh, no!" "She's gonna win!" "He's gonna win!"

They clasped the rails on the ends of the beds and rocked back and forth. Some of them waved their arms or jumped—as much as each could—in excitement.

The racetrack route circled to the back wall and returned to the doorway. The turnaround was the tricky part. Charlene was best at handling her right wheel and she flipped herself with finesse, while George put his competitive experience and greater strength into a spurt of energy for his turn. He only had one good arm, but he was adept at using his one mobile leg to make the pivot. Peter knew how to judge the narrow space. He rolled as close as he could to the wall, and then spun both wheels at the same time, making his chair spin like a top.

Back they all sped, a look of delight and concentration on their faces, the exuberant crowd urging them on. The finish line was in sight—Karen held her crutch high enough above the racer's heads so no one would hit it, while she leaned heavily on the other crutch to stay upright.

As they reached the last leg of the race, George's left wheel rammed into Peter's chair. The crash disrupted their momentum, and they were driven sideways into one of the beds. Charlene soared past Karen's crutch, claiming the win.

"Yahoo," she whispered loudly. The crowd muffled their claps and congratulated her. The next three competitors lined up, with the winner set to compete with Charlene for first prize.

Charlene beamed with pride and flicked her hair back. A few kids who were ambulatory bumped her shoulder. Dale smiled at her and he thought she smiled back. He would have loved to race, to feel athletic again, as if he were flying down the sheet of ice on the sharpest of skates, but his fingers still couldn't grasp the wheels of the chair tightly to propel himself. He envied her.

"Young love. Kissy-kissy."

Dale turned around. It was Lindsay, watching him from his iron lung. "I can see you," he said, gulping air.

Dale looked away.

The second heat lined up. The spectators were rowdier this time, and Karen shushed them before she would let them race. "Be quiet," she whisper-shouted, her index finger bouncing against her lips. "They"ll be here soon to check on us. We have to finish before they come!"

Reluctantly, the crowd calmed down, because from the glare she gave them, Karen clearly wasn't going to lift her crutch until they did. When she dropped it, though, the kids forgot their promise and cheered the racers with gusto. Albert won easily, and got in place for the showdown with Charlene. The final race was two rounds of the track.

Charlene wheeled in beside him and the race began. Albert took an early lead after two beds, but Charlene dug down and caught up. By the time they got to the wall, they were even. Both of them spun around easily and headed on back. On the second round, Charlene made the better turn and got to the wall again before Albert. She tilted on her turn, which cost her a second as her chair righted itself. Her eyes opened wide in surprise, as she shifted her weight to avoid falling over.

Albert seized the moment to zip his chair around and sprint toward the finish line. Charlene recovered, darting up quickly from behind. Albert was caught off guard. Dale could see him trying to keep her in his sights and concentrate on rolling his wheels at the same time. The crowd erupted with "Come on, Charlene," and "Yay, Albert!" Karen stretched up as high as she could to extend her crutch.

It was a near photo-finish, but Albert's footrests crossed the line an inch ahead of Charlene's. The kids laughed uncontrollably and noisily, with Albert raising his arms in victory. Charlene clenched her fists and shook them in mock disappointment, because she was laughing, too. Dale thought again how beautiful she looked, how her eyes twinkled when she laughed. He tried not to, but couldn't help sneaking a glance at Lindsay, whose gaze seemed fixed on Dale, a permanent sneer on his face.

Everyone celebrated, and out of the chatter came the decision to expand the fashion show into a giant talent show for staff and families. The suggestions flew fast and furious—another wheelchair race, a bubble-blowing contest, a marble contest, a choir, a dance troupe, and more.

"Let's call it 'a polio parade,'" one boy suggested. An organizing committee quickly formed. Karen ditched her bossiness and threw in ideas. She and Charlene conferred about the details.

The kids' illegal conspiracy became noisier, as the potential for the show grew in their imaginations until, suddenly, a sharp bark interrupted them: "Hey, something's wrong with George!" someone yelled.

The kids separated to reveal George slumped in his chair, his chest heaving air in and out. His face was paler than usual, his good arm lay limp at his side.

Peter shouted, "Help!" in his loudest voice, and an orderly appeared at the door of the ward to demand, "What's going on here? You're all supposed to be in bed!"

The orderly caught sight of George and bellowed down the hallway, "Emergency!" He rushed over, scooped George out of his chair as if he weighed no more than a feather, and raced out of the ward. The kids watched in stunned silence as they disappeared down the hall.

CHAPTER 10

All the staff on the ward were unusually quiet, while they helped the patients eat and dress the next morning. None of the nurses, nurses' aides, or orderlies made conversation with the kids; none of them even looked them in the eye. The aide making his bed usually greeted Dale with a bubbly "Good morning," and chatted amicably, telling him about the weather and her own small children, inquiring about his well-being. Today, though, she didn't speak, tugging at the starched white sheets as if they were resisting, folding the hospital corners with extra precision, and tucking them tightly under the mattress. He thought maybe he might have offended her, until he saw the same silent treatment going on all down the aisle.

George was back in the iron lung on the ward for the sickest patients. He was sleeping soundly, obviously having suffered a setback. Were the rest of them being punished for having fun, for acting like typical kids for a change? George had likely not been feeling well before the race, but he had gladly participated. He wanted to feel normal, too.

An hour later, Charlene wheeled up to Dale's bed. Her ponytail was pulled tightly, and a silver barrette fixed wayward strands on the side of her head. "What's going on?" she asked, looking down the ward, then at him. "Why are they all so glum?"

Dale pushed the tiddlywinks mat aside. Mrs. Stewart had brought it so he could work on strengthening his fingers. He'd practiced grasping the little disks, pressing them firmly with the black disk—the squidger—to get them to jump into the cup. He'd been writing about his frustrations on a piece of paper, and decided by the end of the paragraph, that his hand must be getting stronger, because his cursive letters weren't half as messy as the first time he tried.

If he focused on getting better, he'd get there, he thought. When he felt discouraged, he pictured himself wrangling his goalie stick, and whapping errant pucks from the air with his gloves. All he had to do was look at how his writing skills had improved to remind him.

"I don't know what's wrong," he said. He sat up straight, tugged the lapels of his bathrobe, and tightened the belt. Miss Nelson, a friendly new nurse, had brushed his hair when he woke up, but he wished he had a mirror to check his appearance. He didn't know what to say to Charlene now. He pulled the mat back in front of him, and shook the tiddlywinks out of the cup.

Charlene smiled at his unease. "You look nice," she said. "You're getting better. Maybe you will get out of here—soon. And maybe I will, too. I have good news. Mrs. Stewart's been making me walk in the handrails— finally! I'm going to try using crutches in a few days." She fairly bounced as she announced her news.

"That's great," he said, but his voice was dull. He busied himself with the tiddlywinks.

"What's wrong?" Charlene asked, sinking back into her chair.

Dale glanced across the aisle to see Lindsay watching them. His shoulders moved up and down as he gulped air, but the work of breathing didn't stop him from staring, and before Dale could look away, Lindsay puckered his lips in a kiss directed at him.

"Nothing," Dale said. "I don't know what's going on. Why don't you go ask someone?" He turned back to his game. One of the winks popped up and landed on the floor near Charlene's chair. She reached down.

"Leave it," he said, his eyes on the mat.

Charlene sat back up. Her smile faded. She waited a moment, then began turning her chair. Morley approached, pushing a cart with fresh sheets, but didn't offer her his usual warm greeting.

She stopped him. "What's wrong with everyone today? Why are you mad at us?" she said, a furrow in her brow.

He paused, then said, "No one's mad at you. Not at all. The news about the vaccine isn't good." He smoothed a ripple on the sheets. "Some kids in California got polio after they were inoculated. Eleven of them have died." He swallowed hard. "They've suspended the program in the U.S. and here in Canada, too." He flicked an invisible piece of dust on the top of the sheets.

Dale had kept his eyes lowered, but he'd listened to every word. The news hit him like a ton of bricks. He looked up. "Why? Why didn't the vaccine work?" he asked.

"They don't know yet," Morley said, drumming his fingers on the sheets. "They don't know. But they're not taking any chances, so no one else is getting it until they figure out what happened."

Charlene drew in a breath. "That's terrible. How about in Canada? Did anyone here get polio?"

"I haven't heard of any." Morley shook his head. "Sorry, we're all a little upset about it. We were hoping the vaccine would bring an end to all of this." He stuck his hands in his pockets; his shoulders fell.

Dale looked down the ward. It seemed so normal now to see kids in iron lungs, wheelchairs, rocking beds, and hobbling on braces and crutches.

"I have to go, kids," Morley said. "Maybe we'll wake up from this nightmare soon." He shook his head, gave the cart a shove, and pushed it out of the ward.

Charlene moved her chair toward Dale again. "What's the matter with you?" She lowered her voice. "I ... I thought we were friends. I ..." she hesitated, "I thought you liked me." Her cheeks were red.

Dale looked to the side. Lindsay was watching them, a smile on his face. Knowing Dale saw him, he drew in some air and puckered his lips at him again.

Charlene yanked the wheel of her chair and caught sight of Lindsay's mocking gesture. When Lindsay saw her, his smile grew wider between gulps of air. She turned back to Dale, clearly shocked.

"Well, you thought wrong," Dale said, doing his best not to look at her. He turned the other way on his bed, his back to Charlene. He flipped another tiddlywink, which flew too far and hit the floor.

He heard her draw in a sharp breath, then wheel herself away.

CHAPTER 11

All the kids needed an hour of rest in the afternoon, whether it was the weight of the shepherd's pie and tomato aspic lunch that had made them sluggish, or the heat pouring in through the giant windows. The orderlies had hoisted them open, but with little wind blowing in, the wards were heating up.

The radio played in one corner, a CBC school broadcast about the history of Confederation playing at a low volume. A few boys sat nearby, listening, while another few down the aisle played cards, chess, or Candyland, an easy board game—each player drew a colored card and moved along the path until the end. One of the children drawn on the playing board had a brace on his leg. The doctors hoped the drawing would make their patients feel more normal. Other kids were visiting their friends' bedsides, when Miss Nelson's voice broke the quiet.

"You have a visitor, Dale." The nurse's cheery voice and wide smile made Dale pull his eyes away from the pale green paint on the wall, squelch his gloomy thoughts, and smile back. He'd been trying to force himself to write out how he could undo the cruel words he'd uttered to Charlene, how he could express his disagreement with his mother's views. For today, that took precedence over his dream of making it back on the team. But nothing came out of his pen; it lay unused on his nightstand; the paper was blank.

"Hello, dear." His grandmother peeked from behind the nurse's shoulder. A blue hat with a jaunty feather of the same color framed her wavy silver hair. "How are you?" she asked, almost timidly, blinking her eyes repeatedly as she asked the question.

His grandmother always complained about being cold, but today she wore only a light sweater—pale blue, he noticed—over her gray and white checkered dress. The scent of perfume surrounded her as usual; he knew each of the handkerchiefs inside her beige handbag always received a drop of her favorite fragrance. Her gloves were white as snow, also as usual. She was beautiful. His mother had been a younger version of her.

She stood at the bottom of his bed.

A feeling of relief washed over him. He was becoming numbed to his father's absence, but now suddenly realized how much he missed his family. Still, the sense of being abandoned when he needed support most had taken root in him. "I'm fine," Dale said, but controlled his voice so he wouldn't appear joyful. His grandmother smiled, wringing her hands together. She didn't move.

At first, he didn't understand her dilemma. Dale saw all the boys focused on his corner, wondering who this person was and what she would do next.

"It's okay, Grandma," he said. "You can't catch polio from any of us on this ward. We're not infectious anymore. Honest. You can come closer."

Grandma's smile seemed stuck in place, but she inched closer along the aisle and sat down on the gray metal chair beside Dale's bed.

"So nice to see you, darling," she said. She didn't pat his hand or hug him. "You're getting better? Are they taking good care of you?" The other boys relaxed and went back to their cards and visiting, but at a quieter volume, to keep an ear on the conversation between Dale and his visitor. The voice on the school broadcast talked about the role of Sir John A. Macdonald and D'Arcy McGee in bringing the four provinces together to form Confederation in 1867.

"Yes, sure. How are you?" Dale searched his mind. There was so much he wanted to ask. He understood why some people might be afraid of polio, but his grandmother was a smart woman who always asked questions. He saw she'd also been affected by irrational fears.

"Well, yes, I'm fine, dear. I've been so concerned about you." She sat back. "I wanted to come earlier, but, well ... all the things I've read ..." Her voice dropped off. She raised her lips in a weak smile. "Tell me how you're doing. You were quite sick at first, you poor thing."

"I guess I'm getting better," Dale said. He didn't know what else to talk to her about, so he told her about his progress, that he'd graduated from the iron lung to the rocking bed, and now could breathe on his own consistently. She shook her head at his story. He told her about the physiotherapy sessions, that he had received a set of braces and was practicing walking. Very soon, he hoped, he would be able to walk independently.

Grandma tipped her head to the right. "You know,

Dale, you look a lot like your father, but you've got your mother's eyes and her smile." She sighed. "I sure miss her, my darling Grace. I never expected to lose my daughter."

She looked down and breathed in and out a few times, then looked up and changed the subject. "Are the nurses nice?" Her smile wobbled a bit, but she continued. "Are they friendly?"

The hour after lunch was a difficult time each day for Dale, as was the nighttime. He could keep thoughts about his mother at bay when he was busy, and the ward was a busy place—meals, physiotherapy, schoolwork, fooling around—but enforced periods of idleness allowed him to see her in his mind, hear her humming in the kitchen. His grandmother's presence reminded him that his mother had died less than five months ago.

His dad's parents lived in Saskatchewan. The families visited back and forth every few years. Dad's parents had taken the train to Winnipeg to attend Mom's funeral and left a few days after. They were loving, but Dale didn't know them as well as he knew his mother's mom, who had been widowed many years earlier, and lived mere blocks away. He realized how very strange it must have been for Grandma. Over and over again on the day of the funeral, he had heard people clucking their tongues, lamenting her grievous loss. "You never expect to bury your child," they repeated.

He could forgive her absence in his time of crisis.

Which was why he felt it necessary to put on his game face. Dale thought about Miss Clements's sour attitude, and the nasty treatment a few of the other staff dished out, but the kindness and encouragement from others—Dr. Barsky, Morley, Miss Nelson, and Mrs. Stewart—made Dale realize how much they cared about the kids and wanted them to get better.

"Yes, sure, Grandma. Everybody's great here."

She lowered her head and nodded toward the other boys. "And the other children?" she asked. "How are they doing, poor souls?"

"They're fine, Grandma," Dale said. "They're fine."

He didn't mention George, who was still in the iron lung in an acute ward. Dale had visited him a few times and they'd talked, but George didn't have much energy, and was clearly frustrated at having to wait for the machine to exhale before he could utter any words. Karen had been there, too, keeping him company, even when he slept. She'd given Dale a pained smile.

"I can tell the nurse if he needs anything," she'd told him. "He choked the other day. He has trouble swallowing, and his food went down the wrong way. It was awful," she'd said, her eyes suddenly welling up.

Dale slipped his eyes to the side to see the other boys on the ward were listening. Finally, he couldn't wait. "How are Dad and Brent? Why hasn't Dad come? Why didn't you come to visit me sooner?"

Grandma cast her eyes down and raised her gloved hands over her eyes. Several moments passed. "What's wrong, Grandma?" Dale blurted out. He began to panic. "What's happened?"

It took his grandmother what seemed to be an even longer time to compose herself. Dale held his breath, his eyes fixed on her gloves. When she moved her hands down, her face was red, and tears had spilled down her cheeks.

"It's ... it's your brother." She choked the words out. "He's got—" and the word fell from her lips as she began to cry "—polio." She covered her face again and wept openly.

Any boys who were talking fell silent. Someone turned the radio off. Dale froze. He couldn't decide if it was right to move, to speak, to breathe.

His grandmother recovered her composure, clicked open her purse, and took out a white cloth hankie. She wiped the tears that streaked her makeup and blew her nose. She looked up at Dale. "I'm so sorry to bring you this news, darling. He got sick last week. He's here, downstairs, on the ward for younger children." She dipped her eyes. "It's been an awful time." She didn't raise her eyes.

Dale's skin broke out in goosebumps. He thought he was shaking.

He could hardly move his jaw to speak. "Brent is here? In the hospital?" he hissed.

She nodded, her eyes still down.

"Why didn't Dad tell me? Why didn't he visit? Why didn't you tell me?" His voice rose now, louder and louder, but was still barely above a whisper.

His grandmother swallowed hard, then looked at him, reaching her gloved hand to grasp Dale's, which lay limp on the bed.

"Your father's a mess, Dale," she said. "He misses your mom. He's trying to hide it by working constantly, then you got sick—and now it's Brent. He brought Brent into the hospital in the middle of the night, then had to go straight to work in the morning. He's been running non-stop—" she squeezed his hand.

"But he hasn't come to see me. You didn't come to see me!" He seethed inside.

"He forbade me to come, and he told the doctors and nurses not to tell you, either." She heaved a sigh, the truth finally unburdening her. She forced a smile, even as tears brimmed in her eyes. Dale forced himself to breathe. He drew his hand back from under hers. He turned his head away to see all the boys watching him, but this time, none of them looked away. They looked as startled as he felt.

Grandma cleared her throat and spoke urgently. "But you're both going to be fine—which is wonderful, isn't it, Dale? Isn't it?" she insisted. "Brent is still in an iron lung, but you were, too, right? And you got out."

He couldn't turn toward her. His goosebumps subsided, the oppressive heat of the room now strangling him. His head throbbed. "Right," he murmured, and closed his eyes.

He didn't know how long she sat there, but after a time, the chair scraped backward; he heard the tap-tap of his grandmother's heels on the linoleum, and her scent gradually disappeared.

He had to remind himself to keep breathing.

CHAPTER 12

They'd added a ward in the basement of the hospital, especially for younger kids, because of the large number of children sick with polio in Winnipeg. Dale supposed separation of the children by age groups, and the constant busy activity of the hospital, had made it easier to keep Brent's presence from him.

He confronted Morley in the hallway. "Why didn't you tell me?" he demanded.

"He was on isolation at first, so you couldn't have seen him, anyway, and they wouldn't let me tell you. He's on the ward now," Morley said. "I'll take you there." He motioned to the elevator.

"No, my legs are getting stronger, and I'd rather do this on my own." Dale insisted. He rolled his wheelchair to the edge of the staircase. He grabbed the bannister, pulled himself up, and began to inch his way down the stairs sideways, one leg at a time.

"Hold it," Morley ordered. "Go down the stairs on your backside. You don't have your braces right now, and you'll wear yourself out before you get there. It's two floors down. Use your rump or it's back to bed with you."

Dale grumbled, but gave in. He'd been getting better and faster on his braces, and was mostly able to walk without crutches. The technician had taken them today to make an adjustment, with the promise to bring them back soon.

"I'm building braces for a lot of kids," he said. "But I'll fix them up as quickly as I can."

Morley helped him inch down the stairs, standing on the steps at the bottom of each flight to make sure he was safe. When he reached the basement, Dale piled into another wheelchair. Morley then pushed him through the big doors.

The yellow walls were decorated with wooden cutouts of ducks and kittens, puppies and chickens scampering along the wall. Morley pushed him past a giant toy box in the corner, a few dolls and cowboy hats piled on top. This room was even noisier than his own ward, filled with the high-pitched voices of younger boys and girls babbling, screeching, and asking for help. It stunned him to see several babies and toddlers in iron lungs, their eyes searching as they puzzled over their strange reality in the monster machines. An aide or orderly stood beside nearly every one. They were talking to the little ones, reading them stories, or reaching into the portals on the side to clean them or massage their distorted muscles.

In the play corner, a toddler with braces on her legs lurched forward, balancing on the handle of a dolly buggy. She looked awfully pleased with herself, with an aide standing behind, holding her hands out to catch her if she fell. A boy, about the same age, poked his fingers on the keys of a small accordion, puzzled at how to get the instrument to produce a sound. He accidentally shifted the bellows, making the instrument bray, but he couldn't connect the action with the music.

For a moment, Dale didn't understand why Morley had stopped. Then he realized why—his brother lay in the iron lung right in front of him. He didn't recognize Brent at first. His hair was plastered back, his skin pale. His head was all that was visible, not the boisterous, round little body that Dale roughhoused with on the bed or the living room carpet on Sunday mornings.

Morley gave Dale a pat on the shoulder and left.

A smile exploded across Brent's face when he saw Dale in his mirror. "Hi, Dale!" he squeaked. Through the glass window, Dale could see Brent's body lying motionless. He also saw that his brother was dressed in pajamas Dale had never seen before, with black, brown, and white horses galloping over the blue material. He supposed they belonged to the hospital and would never make it home to Smithfield Avenue.

"Hooray! I get to see you," Brent squeaked some more. "I missed you."

"What happened?" Seeing his brother this way tore Dale inside.

"I don't know," Brent said, wagging his head. "I got sick in the middle of the night. I was crying and Dad called the ambulance, and they brought me here. I was really, really tired for a couple of days, but now I'm better. It doesn't hurt as much."

"Better? Oh ... that's good, good."

Dale rolled himself closer to make it easier for Brent to see him without looking in the mirror. Brent smiled. "The nurses are really nice, aren't they? I really like Miss Nelson best of all. She gave me ice cream!"

Dale stared at Brent. "Did they tell you when you can get out of the iron lung?" He tried to sound hopeful.

"Uh ... no ..." Brent shook his head. "They didn't tell me yet—"

"Did you get the vaccination at school with the other kids?" Dale blurted. He needed to know. A nurse helping another patient lifted her eyes at his voice.

"Nope." Brent frowned. "Dad wouldn't let me. Remember?"

Dale's heart sank. The morning news broadcast had announced that the government of Canada was renewing the vaccine program. He had listened carefully as Paul Martin, the Minister of Health, spoke:

"I am satisfied that Connaught Laboratories, at present the sole source in Canada of the vaccine, is engaged in doing everything it can to provide a safe vaccine for our children."

Schools in Winnipeg were reorganizing vaccine clinics right away. The American program was still being scrutinized for what had gone wrong there.

"When's Dad coming back?" Brent asked.

"What do you mean?" Dale was angry, not caring

even if other people heard them. "Was he here?"

"He came last night. Didn't he come to see you? He said he would."

Dale needed to leave. He looked behind to see if Morley had returned. Instead, he saw Charlene standing there, black shoes on her feet, braces on her legs, supported by hand crutches. She was watching Dale and Brent.

She walked haltingly over. She must have just been fitted for the crutches. She wasn't good at walking yet, but it was a start.

"That's your brother?" she said.

"Uh ... yeah ... this is Brent," Dale said. "Um ... why are you here?"

"I play with the little kids. I know Brent, don't I?" she said, flashing her smile for the little boy. "Want another story today?"

"Yes, yes!" Brent said. "Read me *Horton Hears a Who* again. Please?"

Charlene laughed. "You like that line, don't you? *A person's a person, no matter how small.*"

"I do. Can you read it?"

"Sure. You visit with Dale right now, and I'll be back

in a few minutes. I'll get some other kids to listen, too."
She turned to walk away.

Dale was overwhelmed with sadness. He turned his chair to her as Charlene moved away. "I'm really sorry," he said. "I didn't mean it."

"Are you?" Charlene turned back slightly. She sniffed. "It wouldn't have worked anyway." She walked away, stiffly but confidently, and bent over carefully to fish a small ball out of the toy box. She waved at a little girl sitting in a wheelchair. Within seconds, they were playing a simple game of catch. Dale could see the girl's hands had also been affected; she couldn't grasp the ball.

To Dale's relief, Morley arrived at that moment to whisk him back to his ward.

"Bye, Dale," Brent called out. Dale waved behind him.

"See you," he replied, without much enthusiasm.

CHAPTER 13

"You're being discharged."

"I'm what?"

Dr. Barsky's giant smile showed how pleased he was. "Tomorrow's Saturday. Your dad will be here to get you."

The news sped down the ward. "Lucky you!" "Congratulations!" "Fantastic news!" "Lucky!"

Dale walked downstairs, slowly, but with straight legs, to tell Brent right away. Two weeks in, his brother was no further ahead. Any efforts to open up the iron lung had failed; Brent couldn't draw a single breath on his own.

"Will you come and visit me?" Brent asked. "I'll miss you." His eyes welled up and his nose turned red.

"Sure, I will. I'm coming for physiotherapy. I'll see you on Monday," Dale said, patting his brother's head lovingly. "I'll visit you all the time. I promise."

"Really?"

"Honest, I promise. Grandma comes all the time, too, doesn't she?" Their grandmother had overcome her fears of the hospital, of catching polio from the kids. She baked sugar cookies, and was now a regular and popular visitor on the ward. "You won't be lonely, you'll see." Dale sighed, desperate that the happy announcement not be any sadder. "How about I read you a story," he said.

"Sure," Brent said. "I guess, but I know all the stories here already."

Dale swallowed hard. He'd hardly read a book with Brent since their mother died, and now Charlene and others had been reading to his brother regularly.

"Well, I don't know them. Maybe if I hold the pages up, you can read them to me. How's that, sport? You're nearly in Grade 2. You have to keep practicing."

Brent lit up at the challenge. "Okay! I can read really big words."

By the time they were done, Brent had read *Madeleine's Rescue* and *The Little Red Caboose*. Dale felt a surge of pride at Brent's willingness to figure out names like "Genevieve." They had a fun visit over the books, talking about how silly Madeleine was to jump into the Seine River just to frighten Miss Clavel, and the bravery of the little caboose that saved the runaway train.

"I miss Mom," Brent said, breathing out hard as Dale closed the last book.

"Me too, squirt."

"She died in the hospital, didn't she?" Brent's voice was gruff, near tears.

"But not this one," Dale assured him. "And you're not going to die. I promise."

"Dad misses her," Brent said, blinking back tears. "He cries at night. He thinks I'm asleep and that I don't hear him, but I do."

"It's hard for him," Dale said. He smoothed Brent's hair.

"Yeah," Brent said quietly. "It is."

Dale kissed Brent on the forehead. "I gotta go, squirt. But I'll be back Monday. Promise. Don't go anywhere without letting me know."

"You're dumb," Brent laughed, back to being six. "You're a big dummy."

Dale climbed back up the steps—going up was harder and his muscles still complained, but he fought his way there, walking slowly down the hall to the ward for the sickest children. The dim lights and the whoosh and hum of the machines reminded him of the critical condition of the patients inside the iron lungs. Nurses and aides buzzed about—checking, fixing, adjusting, helping.

George lay sleeping again, as he had been the last time Dale visited, his head poking out of his iron prison. His hair had grown longer, his cowlick reaching halfway down his cheek. Dale wanted to push it back, so George would look like George again, but he didn't want to wake his friend, who looked exhausted, no matter how much rest he had. He left.

Lindsay didn't have much to say when Dale told him. "Yep, everybody gets out of here finally. Except me." He rocked up and down. "Even your lover-girl is going to be sprung one day. Maybe you'll have a romance after all." He cackled, then coughed. "Kiss, kiss."

Dale had had enough. "You're sickening," he spat at Lindsay. "Sickening!" He turned and walked away.

"Hey, don't go away mad!" Lindsay called out, sarcasm dripping in his voice.

On Saturday, all the kids who could, gathered around him. The hospital laundry had given his clothes a special wash that morning, as proof they were not infected. The soapy smell reminded him of his stinky hockey sweater, and his mother. It made him feel good.

Miss Nelson confiscated his comb. "Sorry," she said. "But you're going home—you'll get another one. Think of it that way. We're so happy for you!"

He'd stowed the few papers he'd been using for his diary in the bottom of his shoe, pressed as flat as possible so he wouldn't limp and reveal his theft. He didn't have anything else to take home.

His paralysis had lifted rapidly, compared to what happened to other kids. He'd only needed braces for a few days before he took a few stuttering steps on his own. He decided he would do whatever it took to strengthen his muscles. After the lights were out, he inched around his bed, holding on to the steel side rails as support. He collapsed on the mattress after the first try, thoroughly spent. The next night he practiced again, and again. Soon he could do it unaided, delighting Mrs. Stewart and the other kids with a surprise demonstration. He had to slow down if he walked too much, but he gained confidence as he gained strength. He'd practiced his finger exercises, too, and could now write decently for a few minutes without resting his hands.

Everyone gave him a rousing send-off. Karen thumped in, Charlene trailing far behind her. They were both still in braces and on hand crutches, their progress halting. Karen gave him a playful knock with her crutch.

"Don't get kissed by too many girls," she ribbed, to lots of guffaws and chortles. Charlene held back in the crowd, looking down at the ground. Dale blushed.

"Don't forget us," one of the boys said.

"I have to come back for physiotherapy," Dale said. "Tell George I said 'hi,'" he told Karen.

His father appeared in the doorway of the ward. He stood ramrod still, his lips tightly set in a line, his arms stiff at his side, with his hat clutched tightly in his left hand.

Dale's eyes met Dad's. Neither of them moved. The kids around them looked back and forth between them. Some of them knew Dale's dad hadn't visited. Some wondered who this man was.

His father strode forward to break the deadlock. "Let's go home," he said, circling his arm around Dale's shoulder. Dale didn't bend into the hug. He turned his eyes and looked down at his father's hand. His dad dropped his arm and cleared his throat. "Whenever you're ready," he said.

Dale walked slowly toward the door of the ward with his dad. He turned back to smile at his friends. "I'll see you Monday. You can't get rid of me. And I want to see the talent show, too." He waved at everyone.

His heart thumping, he left the hospital.

CHAPTER 14

Home now. What had been his goal was now boring, and very lonely.

First, Dale excused his father's silence because it was all so new. As they drove home in the Winocurs' car, Dad mumbled about how useful it would be to have a car of their own. Otherwise, he was largely speechless. The first thing he said when they got into the house was, "Uh ... well, you're home now. Good ... good. Uh ... I ... I'll be outside. The grass needs mowing." He motioned to a small wicker basket with clean laundry next to the chesterfield. "Why don't you work on that? You can sit down while you do it. Put the radio on, if you like." Before he closed the front door, he stopped and said, more to himself, "I suppose we need something for supper. Toasted tomato sandwiches—should be good enough." Then he went outside.

With that, his dad established the new tone of the

household. Dale had wanted to lie down, but instead he paired socks and folded towels. Through the window he watched his father push the hand mower hard, back and forth over their tiny lawn, going over the same rows again and again, talking to himself as the blades spun uselessly above the already cut grass.

Over the next two days, they talked about ridiculously trivial things. Not once did Dad ask him about how he had felt being sick, what he did in the hospital, how he felt now. Not once did he mention Brent's tragic circumstances or what the future might hold for him. Washing the dishes and sweeping the kitchen floor seemed to be the important topics for Dad.

The alarm rang on Monday morning. "Dale!" His father's voice boomed from the kitchen. "I'm leaving for work now. The porridge is on the stove."

Dale groaned and plumped his pillow. He reached over to the window blind and pulled it up. The bright June sun made the world look perfect. The fresh air wafted in through his window screen.

His dad called out, "Don't forget to wash your dishes." Then the back door clapped shut.

He checked his alarm clock: 7:40 AM. It took Dad all

of five minutes to walk to the Roco station, but he liked to "shoot the breeze" with the other mechanics before they started engine repairs at 8. Dale hoped Dad had more to say to his workmates than he did to his son.

What would his mother have done if she were still alive? His mother—his mother. Dale fell back on his pillow. She would have visited him in the hospital. She would have been excited at his progress. She would have told him she loved him. She would have worried about Brent. But Dad had done none of these things.

He hauled himself out of bed and did his exercises right away—heel raises, deep knee bends, touching his toes, clenching his fingers—as best he could. He missed the hospital more than he thought he would. He'd become used to the routine, the flow of people, and the constant hubbub.

The busy-ness of the hospital made him sleep well at night. On the first night home, he had a nightmare. In it, he was trapped in an iron lung, with the collar too tight around his neck, strangling him, and he was unable to free himself. He called out but his voice croaked, and no one came to help.

He woke, sweating and panting for air, then fought

sleep until exhaustion overtook him. He'd had the same nightmare last night, too.

Now it was morning and he could avoid the dream, even though it was at the back of his mind. He tried writing about it in his journal, but all sorts of emotions bothered him when he did, so he stopped trying to figure it out.

Alone in the house, there was a silence even the radio couldn't pierce. He kept hearing his mother's voice, singing along with it. He decided he had to think ahead, to work at getting back to normal, planning for hockey tryouts.

He got ready for the day, spooning porridge into a bowl with a yellow and white plaid pattern. His mother had bought the set of dishes at Eaton's department store. Yellow was her favorite color. "Like the sun," she'd said.

The brown sugar didn't melt on the cooled sludge, and the milk merely sat on top of the cereal. At least the porridge at home was the same as in the hospital, he thought ruefully. He made a mental note to read the instructions on the bag of oatmeal to see if he could make a decent pot himself. He took the bowl outside and sat down on the steps, swirling the spoon around to mix the sugar in. The sunlight warmed the air. Robins sang out in the trees.

Kids emerged from their houses, heading to school in the gorgeous last week, excited about summer vacation, but jabbering about what might happen come September. Girls skipped and boys jumped around as they greeted their friends. Dale smiled at the memory of joining up with the stream of children going to Seven Oaks School. He and Paul had had a lot of fun every day when they were little, in the simple act of walking to school.

When he turned from watching the little ones, he realized Paul was there—walking up Smithfield, on the way to their class at Edmund Partridge. Two other boys from school chummed with him. They were laughing loudly, and all talking at the same time. Then Paul saw him.

"Hi," Paul called, raising a hand, a surprised note in his voice. He stopped at the bottom of the walk that led to Dale's door. The other boys waved at Dale. Paul indicated he'd catch up, and the other two carried on, looking back at Dale, clearly talking about him as they left.

Paul shifted the books on his hip. "You're home!"

"Yep," Dale said, dabbling the spoon in his porridge and nodding. "How's everything?"

Paul kicked his heel against the sidewalk. "Everything's fine," he said. "Great. Mr. Leah will be really happy to know you're okay." He stopped. "Are you ... okay?" He still hadn't taken any steps closer.

"Yeah, but not ready for school yet," Dale said. "I have to wait for the doctor to tell me if it's okay to go back. Polio is lousy," he said. "I have to have more stamina to walk that far and get through a day. Soon." He patted the spoon on top of the cereal. "Still moving to your grandparents'?"

"Ah ... probably. Not entirely sure, but probably," Paul said, looking up the street as he answered. "Look, Dale, I couldn't visit—"

"Yeah, yeah, I know. You're not sixteen yet."

"And I'm a terrible letter writer." He changed the subject. "Hey, what about school? How are you going to pass?"

"They have a teacher in the hospital," Dale said. "I'm going to go for physiotherapy a few times a week, so I'll see her then. She has all the assignments from class, and she's worked it out with the school. They've told me I'll pass." He took a small bite of the cold porridge, which gurgled on the way down.

"Great," Paul said. He still hadn't moved. "Dale," he said. A robin chirped.

"Yeah, I know. Your parents don't want you to come near me, right?" He thought about the hugs Paul's mother had given him in the past. There would be no more hugs, he expected.

Paul sighed audibly and stuck his free hand in his pants pocket. A skiff of breeze tossed his hair. He pulled his hand out of his pocket and tapped his hair down. "Yeah, I'm sorry. My mom's going to send over soup and dumplings, but she's scared of polio. Until I get a vaccination, I can't go near you."

An awkward silence ensued, lasting several seconds. "You didn't tell Mr. Leah you're moving?" Dale asked.

"Uh ... well, I'm not sure ... uh ... I don't know," Paul said, stubbing his toe on the ground. "My dad says we'll see ... I don't know," he stumbled.

"Do you think you're being fair to the team?" Dale asked. Paul's selfishness miffed him. "Mr. Leah needs to know, in case he has to find another starting goalie."

"What, don't you think you'll be ready to play? I need to know." Paul's tone was urgent.

"'Course, I'm going to try," Dale said. He tapped his

spoon on the edge of his bowl. "They said I'm fine, that I should exercise to get my strength back, that I'll probably be on the ice this fall. But ... what if I can't be? Don't you think he should know, so he can plan for the team?"

"Well, I need to know what you're doing." Paul stood rigidly straight and spoke quickly. "Because I need to plan. You'd do the same thing if it were the other way around. It's not only about the team, but about whether an agent will look at you. Don't pretend it's not."

Dale felt like he'd been slapped in the face. "That's mean, Paul. We always cared about the team. Both of us."

"That's easy for you to say," Paul retorted. "You were always the starter."

One of the boys called down the sidewalk. "Hey, Alexander, let's go!"

Paul waved at the boys. "Coming," he said, then turned to Dale. "I've got to catch those guys or I'll miss the bell."

"Sure," Dale said, getting up from the stair and reaching for the door handle. Paul moved on, and Dale went through the door and didn't look back.

He plunked the bowl of sticky porridge on the counter and flopped down on the chesterfield.

CHAPTER 15

He couldn't believe he'd be relieved to return to the hospital, but as soon as he entered the doors, the tension rolled off him. The smell of disinfectant and fresh wax assailed his nose. He smiled for the first time in two days.

He fairly bounded into the ward, if walking carefully could be considered running. "Hi, everyone," he nearly shouted. The aides and orderlies were cleaning up the table trays after breakfast. The dirty dishes clunked and crashed into steel bins, the cutlery jangling as they pushed the carts along. The staff flashed smiles, then got back to their work. He saw they'd had porridge for breakfast, too. Likely as cold as his was, he thought, by the time it arrived and got doled out.

Most of the kids greeted him warmly. He approached them to chat, noticing right away that another boy had already taken his bed. To his relief, Lindsay was away working with Mrs. Stewart. Other kids were on the way to class or to physiotherapy and, suddenly, there wasn't much to talk about. After a few moments of awkwardness, Dale decided to see Brent before his own exercise session.

Despite being trapped in an iron lung, the little boy perked up when he saw his big brother. He needed to share a secret. "Miss Nelson's really pretty," Brent whispered, and Dale agreed. The nurse's dark, stylish curls framed her face nicely under her nursing cap, and she gave each child a special knowing wink when she helped them.

She worked on the little kids' ward all the time now. Her smile was infectious, and Dale could see her positive effect on Brent. She told knock-knock jokes that made Brent laugh. He declared he made up his own joke to stump her.

"Listen," Brent insisted. "Knock, knock."

"Who's there," Dale replied.

"Boo."

"Boo who?" Dale recalled thinking the same joke was funny when he was in Grade 1.

"Why are you crying?" Brent chortled at his own brilliance.

Brent filled Dale in on what was going on in the hospital. The little kids were going to be treated to a puppet show in the coming days, and a school choir would be coming that afternoon. "They said we can sing with them," Brent said, taking a big gulp of air.

"You're going to sing?" Dale asked. He chucked Brent's chin with his knuckles, admiring his brother's courage. "Sounds like fun."

"Dr. Barsky taught me how to play chess," Brent went on. "Now I know all the moves. I can see the board in the mirror. I tell him what I want to do, and he puts the piece on the square. I already beat him—fair and square!"

"Wow, that's great, Brent." Dale ramped up his enthusiasm. "Why don't you teach me how to play. I've been so busy with hockey, I've never learned. We can play together."

Brent became the coach and they played a game, with Brent defeating Dale easily.

"I think about where the pieces are, and what would happen if they moved to different squares," Brent confided. "That's how I find the best move. It's sort of like hockey. It's fun!"

"Whoa, you're good!" Dale said. "Maybe Dr. Barsky will teach you even more."

"He's not here," Brent said. "Miss Nelson said he won't be here for a while."

"How come?"

"I don't know." The little boy shook his head. "Beats me."

Dale found a children's novel on the shelf and read out a few chapters of *Henry Huggins* by Beverly Cleary. Brent was a good listener, and laughed at Henry's escapades with his dog, Ribsy.

"I gotta go now, squirt," Dale said, ruffling Brent's hair. "See you soon."

"Maybe I'll see you at home," Brent said. "Maybe in a few days!" Miss Nelson was working with the child next to Brent. Dale noticed she was listening and bit her lips tightly at that sunny prediction.

Dale didn't have to endure the horrid wool wrappings in physiotherapy anymore. He'd brought his swimming trunks and climbed into a huge tank of warm water. The smell of chlorine rose from the tank, as moisture dripped down the tiles on the walls; he couldn't help but lie back and relax, while a physiotherapy assistant eased his legs left and right in scissor kicks, then bent his knees, stretching his muscles as far as they would allow. She swooshed his arms from side to side. For a moment, with his eyes closed, he felt like an ordinary kid, forgetting he'd ever been in this polio predicament.

When it came time to exercise, he added extra energy to impress Mrs. Stewart. "Slow down," she said. "Don't worry, lad, you'll be out on the ice next winter." She gave him a few more stretches to include in his home program.

He was glad to be finished quickly. He looked into the intensive care ward. George was awake, looking past the mirror. He raised his eyebrow when he noticed Dale.

"You need a haircut," Dale joked, lifting up the long strand of black hair.

George smiled. "Maybe I should get a buzz cut after all," he gulped in time to the machine. He cleared his throat. "It would be easy to take care of." A strip of tissue paper hung from the mirror, put there to see how much air George expelled. It fluttered, but barely. He cleared his throat again and gulped. Dale pulled his chair close to the iron lung and his friend.

The conversation was short. George didn't have much interest in the sports news Dale had collected. "You'll be skating again next season, won't you? Not me," George said finally. "I'm done for. It's getting worse every day."

"Don't say that."

"It's okay," George said. He stared past the mirror again. "My parents come in as often as they can. You know what that means. They're not putting all that effort into seeing me during the growing season to make small talk. They're in pieces, and so am I." He paused, gulping air. "My brother hates school. Poor guy! Now he'll have to study math, or the farm will go broke." He made a momentary effort to smile.

"Don't talk like that," Dale said.

"Let me guess—you probably had the same thoughts, didn't you?" George said. "But you got better, which is great. These Emerson machines have saved a lot of lives." Dale looked at the metal label on the front of George's and every other kid's ventilator. Countless children rescued from certain death would remember that name for the rest of their lives.

"But I'm not getting better." George paused to rest for several moments. He gulped. "This is too awful. I'm helpless and I'm useless." He shifted his eyes to Dale and gulped again. "Just talking to you is wearing me out." He gave Dale a weak smile. "I gotta rest," he said, while the machine whooshed in and out. He closed his eyes.

Mrs. Winocur was due to collect Dale at 11:30, to get him home in time for lunch. Luckily, his neighbors weren't afraid of people recovering from polio. Mr. Winocur went to work in a carpool, and Mrs. Winocur insisted she would ferry Dale to the hospital most days, at least, until he was stronger. "If the car is here," she said, "it's no problem at all." She also promised to give him a cooking lesson that afternoon. She was making cabbage rolls with a pineapple tomato sauce, the same way his mother did. He missed them.

He had his schoolwork under his arm, but he wanted to be alone. He knew kids were busy with their activities all morning, so the sunporch would be empty. He decided to wait in there for forty-five minutes, until Mrs. Winocur arrived to pick him up.

But when he rounded the corner from the stairs, he encountered Charlene, the one person he did not want to see. She sat crumpled in a chair, the braces on her legs forcing them straight ahead, her hand crutches lying awkwardly on each side. Her shoulders were slumped and she looked listless. Her swollen eyes showed she'd been crying. When she saw Dale, she hardly moved.

"Oh," Dale said. He was shocked at her appearance. Something was terribly wrong. He had intruded at an unhappy time. He wanted to flee.

She breathed out and looked away. "You! Hmph ... well, you caught me," she said.

"Sorry? What do you mean?" he asked.

"If you must know, feeling miserable and full of pity for myself," she said.

He felt caught, not wanting to pry, but he knew he'd appear unfeeling if he didn't acknowledge her distress. He stood stock still.

"Do you want me to leave?" he asked.

She breathed again and pulled herself up a bit. Her tone wasn't unfriendly, but it was cool. "No, it's okay. I have to make a decision." She gave a semi-laugh. "I'm still a kid. I don't want to make decisions! But ... I guess I have to." She shifted her eyes to gaze out the window.

"What ... what decision?"

"An easy one and a hard one," she sniffed. She finally pulled herself all the way up, straightened her legs, and rested her crutches against the arm of the chair. She wiped her cheeks where the tears had flowed. "Did you start your new physiotherapy program today?" she asked.

He told her he had.

"That's great. I think I'll be able to go home soon, too, so the hospital is really putting pressure on my parents to send me to a foster home. They said they're trying to help. Trying to help." She blew air out in a gust. "They say that's the way I can have a better chance to be a nurse and have a better life. My parents said they won't stop me, if I think I'll do better without them."

"Whoa," Dale said. "That's awful!"

"Yep," Charlene replied, a bitter tone in her voice. "Awful. I guess you don't have anyone telling you that you have to go live somewhere else because your mother died, do you? The city wants to sell the land we live on to build more new houses, and they won't let us stay. Not us, not my grandparents, not any of my relatives, no one. So, my mom and dad are a wreck over that and a wreck over me."

Dale sat mute.

She blew out more air and rubbed her cheeks again. "They want to fight it, but they can't afford to hire a lawyer and go to court. They don't really have a choice, at all. But," she said, "maybe that's the way I'll get to stay with my family—my parents, at least."

"What do you mean?" Dale asked.

"Well, if they have to move, then the hospital can't make a big deal about our house being too small for me, and not having running water and all that. They're looking for an apartment or a duplex." She shrugged. "They're trying to find something for Grandma and Papa, too, but they don't think we'll live close together, like we do now. I don't know where we'll all end up."

"So," Dale asked carefully, "what's your choice?"

She scowled. "For me, there is no choice. No choice at all." She angled her body to the right, and pushed against the arm of the chair to hoist herself up, then balanced on her crutches. "I guess I can make decisions, even if I am a kid. Sorry for telling you this. See you, maybe," she said, shifting her weight, lifting each leg deliberately.

"There you are!" Mrs. Morris's laugh echoed through the hallway behind him.

Dale spun around. "I knew I'd find you." His teacher clutched three textbooks in her arms, one of them with a ruler peeking out of the cover. She pulled it out. "Don't we have work to do? Hello, Charlene," she said. "I'll see you later, all right?"

Before Dale could say a word, Charlene said, "Yep, after lunch." She swung her crutches around and said, "Bye, Dale," and trundled out of the sunporch. Dale hoped she would turn around, but she kept going.

"Are you ready?" Mrs. Morris asked.

"Uh ... yes," he said, and opened his scribbler to find the final copy of his essay. She tucked it into her books.

"So, what do you think about the information you found?" she asked. They moved out of the sunporch into the hall.

He shook his head to try and clear his mind about what Charlene had just said. "Uh, well, I can't believe people were willing to let smallpox go on killing millions, because they were afraid to learn something new. Nothing showed the vaccine was dangerous—ever. They made it all up. What were they trying to prove?"

"Superstition and imagination are strong drivers, Dale," Mrs. Morris said, "and often greed, if someone had a fake cure to sell. I'm looking forward to reading your essay. Now," and she fumbled through her papers, "take these math questions home. And tomorrow," she tapped his hand with the ruler, "don't leave without seeing me."

"Okay," Dale said. Then, as they both turned down the staircase, he asked, "Mrs. Morris, can I ask you a question? Have you ever heard of Rooster Town? Do you know where it is?"

Mrs. Morris slowed her descent on the stairs. "That's where Charlene lives, isn't it?" A small smile lifted at the corner of her mouth. "Actually, it's not terribly far from here. Off Grant Avenue," she said, pointing west of where they were. She looked at him. "Is that it? Is that all you wanted to know?"

Dale fought to keep it inside, but he had to ask. "Is it okay to like someone, even if they're not the same as you are? What do you think?" The knot that had been clenching in his stomach relaxed as soon as the words were out.

"Oh, good grief, come with me," she said, taking Dale by the elbow and leading him down the stairs and out the hospital door. Her blonde hair gleamed in the light of the sun.

"What awful things have you been listening to?"

He confessed that Lindsay's taunts had intimidated

him, and that he had treated Charlene badly because of them.

"Do you like her or don't you?" Mrs. Morris asked. She tilted her head and put her free hand on her hip.

He shrugged his shoulders. "Yes," he said. "I do, but she doesn't want to have anything to do with me now."

"Well, if she doesn't, you'll have learned a lesson." She put her hand on his arm. "Listen," she said. "You should be proud of the person you like, and they should be proud of you. If you like Charlene, then you should stand up for her." She paused. "But if you decide to be boyfriend and girlfriend, let me tell you that there will be a lot of people making comments because she's a different color."

Dale looked down and kicked the sidewalk with his toe. "I messed that up," he said. "I let Lindsay get to me."

"I can't explain why people are so afraid of each other, but it's as if the color of their skin or their religion determines whether or not they'll be a good person. The funny thing is—the people who make those comments are either mixed up, or aren't good people themselves."

Dale kicked the sidewalk again, whispering his confession, "My mother didn't think people should mix together."

Mrs. Morris clicked her tongue. "Well, I'm sorry you didn't have a chance to discuss it with her," she said, "but whose happiness matters here?"

"She said if people who are different have kids, they won't know where they belong."

"Well, kids belong to their family—and to other good people. If they're not perfect enough, then they probably didn't want to have much to do with that person to begin with."

Dale looked down the broad sidewalk to Osborne Street. A light breeze relieved the heat from the overhead sun.

Mrs. Morris broke the silence. She tapped Dale on the top of the head with her ruler. "I'd love to stay outside and chat all day, but I have children to teach. Got to go." Then she added, "I think I may have to have a few words with Lindsay, too."

At that moment, Mrs. Winocur drove up. Mrs. Morris turned to go back into the hospital. "Don't forget to do your math," she said, and climbed back up the stairs to the hospital.

He got into the car. "How was your morning, Dale?" Mrs. Winocur asked, flashing a bright smile, as she signaled her intention to pull into traffic. "Are you ready to tie on your apron this afternoon?"

"Sure," he said. "I have homework, too." He did have homework to do, he thought, some on paper, some in his soul. The on-paper assignment was far easier.

CHAPTER 16

Before he left the house, Dale checked for the streetcar tickets in his pocket. He'd used their new telephone to call the transit system and ask directions for getting to Hector Street.

His leg muscles didn't hurt when he walked at a normal pace. He was growing stronger, bit by bit, and he wanted to use his time alone during the day for special purposes. At the top of his mind, he wanted to see Rooster Town and find out what was so different about the way Charlene lived.

This was the first day he didn't have to go for physiotherapy. Mrs. Stewart said he was doing well, and he could exercise at home between visits. He told Dad he'd take advantage of the glorious sunny morning to go for a long walk—but he didn't say where, or that he'd also be taking a streetcar and a bus.

He planned his trip so he would be home by noon.

Mrs. Winocur said she'd be home later, and he could come by to learn a few cooking tips. Dad had taken to buying peanut butter, cans of salmon, macaroni, and eggs for quick meals. Grandma had sent over some liver and onions, a roast chicken, and some cookies, but she couldn't make them a meal every day. He missed his mother's cooking—pancakes for weekend breakfasts, Swiss steak, hamburgers, or casseroles for dinner. He was sure his dad would be less grumpy if supper were ready when he came home, and if the meal looked more appealing than a peanut butter sandwich. Dale knew he'd be happier, anyway.

To avoid his father and the other mechanics, who were often milling outside the Roco station, he tucked down a side street and walked a few blocks, before heading up to Main Street and crossing over to catch the streetcar. The humming of the overhead wires reminded Dale of the continual murmuring of the iron lungs. He kept his eye on the stops, and transferred downtown to one of the new buses that ran on diesel gas instead of electricity from wires, riding it out to Grant Avenue. The bus driver dropped him off at Rockland Street.

"The address you want will be a few blocks up there,"

the bus driver told him, pointing to his left. Dale stepped down and the bus rumbled off.

Before crossing the street, Dale looked to the right. On that side of Grant, he saw even lines of small, tidy homes built after World War II. Some houses had shrubs in front, with irises and other spring flowers growing from the earth under windows. A few new trees had been planted on the boulevard, but there were no big shade trees. His parents had told him they'd considered buying a house on these streets when they got married. The government handed out cheap loans to men who had served in the war, and his dad had been in the Air Force. But his grandmother lived in an apartment on Cathedral Avenue in the north end of the city. His mom wanted to be close to her, and his dad had agreed. They had settled several blocks further north.

But the houses he saw as he crossed the street weren't cookie cutter. They sat on bigger plots of land, not regularly spaced, each individually built and looking different from the others. A few were family-sized like his house, while a few others were tiny, like shacks, with sloped roofs. The houses went on for a distance.

Outhouses perched at the back of each property, with narrow paths leading to them.

The sun was higher in the sky now, and it beat down on his head as he walked. Lines of newly planted vegetables poked their tops out of rows in large gardens. Wider paths rather than streets separated the homes. Clusters of bushes and trees dotted the area. A few cars were parked beside houses, but there were no gravel roadbeds to prevent them from getting stuck in wet weather.

Two little boys played in a yard. Crouched in front of piles of earth, they were poking holes in the mud with tiny branches and flicking it in the air. The boys had toothy smiles and the same black hair and brown skin as Charlene. But she'd said she had sisters, so these kids belonged to other families. The front door to one of the houses was open, and the kids ran in and out. He could hear a woman's voice calling from inside.

A bark made him turn. A big tan and white collie stood his ground, perking up his ears at the new person in the neighborhood. Then it sat down quickly to attack an itch, its thick fur jiggling as it scratched its ear with its paw. It stood back up and approached Dale slowly, wagging its tail and accepting a pat. Satisfied, it veered off to snuffle further.

"Can I help you? Looking for someone?" A man hauling a pail of water stopped on the way into his house. He wore blue jeans and a plaid shirt, like Dale's father wore when he was working around the house.

"The Arcand family," Dale said hesitantly. "Do you know them?"

The man chuckled and switched the pail to his other hand. "Of course. We're cousins." With his free hand, he indicated a house not far from where they were standing. "They live over there—the one with the red shingles. You a friend of Charlene's? She's still in hospital. Been there a long time." He moved to open his door.

"Is she ... coming home soon?" Dale asked, nervously. He could feel sweat beading on his forehead.

The man paused. "Oh, I don't know about that. I hear they're making it hard for the family." He turned the knob and pushed the door open. "You know them?"

"Uh ... Charlene," he said. "From ... the hospital." He felt uncomfortable for trying to peer into Charlene's life. "Well, thanks," he said, making to leave.

"Hold on," the man said. "You look hot." He reached

inside his doorway to find a glass and dipped it into the pail. He squinted up at the sun. "I don't think anyone's home right now. The missus took the other kids to school, and she usually buys her groceries in the morning." He held out the glass. "It's getting warm. Drink this before you go," he said and handed it to Dale.

"Oh," Dale said, suddenly realizing he wouldn't have known what to do if Charlene's mother were home. He took the glass and drank the water greedily.

"Should I tell them you were here?" the man asked.

"No!" Dale almost gasped, handing back the glass. "No, that's okay. I ... I can come back. Thanks for the drink," he said, trying to look nonchalant, but sure he was sweating more.

"Okay, suit yourself," the fellow said, and went inside his house.

Dale was getting tired, but he walked over to look at Charlene's house. It was wood clad, not stucco or covered in siding, as most of the houses on the other side of Grant Avenue or in his neighborhood were. The windows were small, two on each side of the front door, covered with blinds to keep the heat of the day out.

It was smaller than his house, which, until his mother died, held four people, with a small bedroom each for Dale and Brent. But Charlene said she had three sisters, plus her mom and dad, so the spaces would certainly be tighter. A wheelchair wouldn't fit, but he was sure Charlene could move around with her hand crutches, even in winter when everyone stayed inside. He shuddered at the idea of someone else deciding where she should live. He wondered who made those decisions, but he came to the conclusion that her family was probably singled out because of where they lived, and because of their skin color.

The Arcand family's home might not be fancy, Dale thought, but home was home. He also sensed that anyone with more money probably had more power, and, with the clout of the city behind them, would get what they wanted. Charlene and her family—the man who was their cousin and all the others—wouldn't be able to afford to challenge the decision, and they would be forced to move wherever they could, but not necessarily together. Dale couldn't imagine being forced to move because someone pushed them out.

He wanted to see how Charlene lived, but his

curiosity had been an intrusion. He walked slowly back to Grant Avenue.

He got on the bus, his legs now worn out. Flopping down onto an empty seat, he shoved the window open to catch the breeze. He'd stuck the papers he'd written on in the hospital into his diary. Since he'd come home, he'd written a few times, but his entries had been listless, without much enthusiasm.

Trying to figure out why Mom died isn't as easy as drawing a sketch of hockey play, and why did I think it would be? I can't figure out what to do, no matter how much I write. And I can't find a solution to the mess I made with Charlene.

And that was it. The nib of the pen sat touching the paper, but he couldn't make it move further, so finally, he fitted the cap on and put it aside.

Maybe chopping vegetables and stirring a sauce would distract him from the shame he felt.

CHAPTER 17

"Let's get the fence fixed this morning."

Dale swallowed the bite of toast he'd just chewed. He put the rest of the piece on the plate. "But Dad, let's take it easy for a few hours. Can we do it this aft—"

"Never mind!" his father growled, tossing back the last drop of coffee in his cup. "Stop this 'I'm sick' garbage." He got up and put his cup in the sink. "Lots of people get sick, but they get back to normal. How old are you? You wanted to be a hockey star, but you can't stand a little work around the house?"

"I'm not lazy, but I'm not supposed to work all the time. You know that!"

"Act like a man, for goodness sakes. There's work to do around here, and I've got to get to the hospital today, too. When have I had the luxury of doing nothing? Come on, let's get the day going."

Dad tromped out the door to the backyard. Dale

could hear him pounding his hammer against the nails. He'd heard Dad pounding his pillow during the night, so Dale was sure the fence was also bearing the brunt of his misery.

He had to escape. He went out the front door and down the steps where he had parked his bike the night before. He felt bad, but he had to get away from his father for a while. He would endure his yelling later. Dale didn't mind helping, but since he'd come home from the hospital, it seemed that his father was bent on proving that there was nothing wrong with him. He was getting better, but he wasn't all there yet, and what was his father trying to prove, anyway?

He had asked his grandmother to intervene, but she'd sighed. "I'll try speaking to him, dear," she said, smoothing his hair, "but he doesn't seem to be listening these days. These things aren't easy, you know." She gave him a weak smile.

Whatever she'd said to his dad had only made him angrier. He was always aggravated. Dale had made his first complete meal a few days ago—Sloppy Joes. Mrs. Winocur had given Dale her recipe and he'd followed it precisely. He'd taste-tested it several times to make sure the balance of ketchup, brown sugar, and mustard was perfect, and it was. A recipe he'd noticed in the newspaper brought back memories of his mom's chocolate chip oatmeal cookies. He thought he might try it and take a few to surprise Brent.

He'd spooned the meat sauce over a round bun, copying the picture in the magazine, but his father hadn't noticed. He'd washed up and changed from his work coveralls when he got home from work, and sat down to dinner. He ate, without asking how it got on his plate or commenting on the taste.

"I'm going to see Brent tonight," Dad said, finishing his glass of water and checking the clock above the kitchen counter. "I have to catch the streetcar at 5:45. Clean up here, will you, and don't forget to sweep the floor."

He didn't notice that Dale hadn't yet touched his food, waiting for his dad to comment on the special meal and how it tasted.

Today had been much the same. Dale had had enough.

Biking was easy on his legs, and he thought it was making them stronger. His feet pushed against the pedals. Biking made him feel normal, like it did when he was younger, pretending to fly through the air. The breeze through his hair refreshed him, the flapping of his pants on his legs reminded him how he had missed his regular activities.

The bike seemed to know where he wanted to go. Before he knew it, he was at the community center, the wooden building that used to be his home away from home.

The boards around the skating rink needed a paint job, he noticed. Grass grew in clumps in the middle of the rink area, struggling after a winter of being covered by ice, but never giving up. He laid his bike on the dirt near the door of the center, which was open. He peeked into the dark hallway. The door to the equipment closet hung open, and from inside, Dale heard items being shuffled, and a familiar voice grumbling to no one.

"Mr. Leah," he called and started down the passage. "Mr. Leah, it's me—Dale!"

Mr. Leah leaned backward from inside the closet. "Dale! Look at you!" He tossed whatever he was holding back into the closet, and grabbed Dale in a huge bearhug. "You're better!"

"Almost ... I'm working really hard at it," Dale said.

A surge of relief coursed through him, the worry that the coach would reject him washing away. "I really am," he said.

Mr. Leah led Dale out into the sunlight. "I understand you were paralyzed," Mr. Leah said, raising his brow, "and in an iron lung."

"But I'm better now, really. I rode here on my bike, and I'm exercising every day. I'm going to be ready for the season." He held his breath.

Mr. Leah leaned against the boards. "Are you sure, Dale? It sounds as if you were quite sick. Do you think you can be as good or better than you were before?" His smile had disappeared; he was talking business.

He was talking about Dale's future, and Dale would not be deterred by his father, polio, or Mr. Leah's fears. "Yes," he declared, trying to tamp down his frustrations. On the one hand, his father wanted him to be better immediately, and now his coach didn't believe he could recover. "They told me there's nothing I can't do, and I'm proof of it! I'm doing everything at home, too. Watch me," and he ran into the middle of the rink. "Look," he cried, raising his arms. His adrenalin surged, and for a few moments he did feel normal. "Look at me. I'm fine!"

He swung his arms a few times and jogged around the rink area. He deked from side to side, throwing his arms and head in the opposite direction.

Mr. Leah burst out laughing. "Take it easy. Tryouts aren't until November," he said. Dale left the rink, Mr. Leah thumping him on the shoulder as he did. "Look, keep your routine up and we'll try you out. Maybe Paul can substitute—"

Dale stopped. "Paul?" he asked. "I thought—"

"Well, things are up in the air about Paul," Mr. Leah interrupted, his finger tapping against the top of the railing. "He really should make up his mind. But even if he stays, he has to try out, as do you. On paper, you look good, but there are the new kids who want the same thing. Fair is fair, Dale. You're competing, remember?"

Everything around Dale felt louder, bigger, harsher. The slight breeze felt like a wind, the hot sun burned until goosebumps prickled his arms. He pushed the long sleeves on his shirt up his arms. He was sweating.

"I have to go," he said quietly. He leaned down and picked up his bike. Swinging his leg over the center bar suddenly seemed like an effort.

"Keep up the good work," Mr. Leah said, frowning,

and walking over to where Dale stood with his bike. "It's not really any different than any other year, is it? You've always had to try out against other players."

"I guess," Dale said. His energy was spent, but he couldn't admit it. He pushed on the pedals and advanced slowly over the mud. "Thanks, Mr. Leah. I'll see you."

He'd escaped from home, and now he had to escape his home away from home. He didn't know where he belonged.

CHAPTER 18

The crowd gathering in the hallway for the talent show made Dale realize how many mothers, fathers, and other family members were connected to all the patients in the hospital. Enough to populate a small town, he thought—so many people affected by polio in one way or another. On the way into the hospital, he and his father had stopped to add their names to a telegram being sent to Dr. Jonas Salk in the United States, to thank him for developing the polio vaccine, for saving lives, and saving children from the danger of paralysis.

"We Love You, Dr. Salk," it read.

Peter was at the table, taking names. "They're collecting names all over the city," he told Dale. "I measured the space each name takes up on a telegram. If people keep signing, we'll have enough names at the end of today to make the telegram seventy yards long—almost as long as a football field. Pretty amazing, isn't it?"

Dale was impressed. He wished the letters could be bigger, to express the emotion in that short sentence.

In the hallway, parents sat with their children on chairs that had been carried from the wards, while others stood at the back. Patients in wheelchairs taking part in the show took up space in the front. Most of them were dressed for the special event. Some hospital staff, including Mrs. Morris, moved about, helping kids. The iron lungs were set at angles along the walls so the kids in them could see, the electrical cords leading to the wall plugs taped firmly to the floor, to prevent anyone from tripping and cutting off the power supply. Lindsay was propped up in a bed on the other side of the hallway, no smile on his face, only a look of resignation as he concentrated on his breathing.

Dale and Dad stood on either side of Brent's iron lung. Eight hockey cards now circled his head, the newest ones sent by his Grade 1 class as a "get well" gift. Dale and Dad placed their hands on top of the machine.

Brent seemed oblivious to the unusual way they were comforting him. "When's it going to start?" he demanded. "Hey, Dad," Brent said, when the show wasn't starting fast enough. "Wanna hear a knock-knock joke?"

There was a whir of anticipation for the show. After what seemed far too long a wait, Karen teetered out of the ward into the middle of the hallway. She still walked tentatively; Dale could see she had made a little progress, but less than she had hoped. Her cheeks flushed red when she saw him, and her smile disappeared for a moment. She lifted her hand slowly and waved at him. He went up to greet her.

"You're so much better," she declared, "It's taking me so long! I want to be able to walk to school in September, but I can't carry anything if I have to use hand crutches. It's so annoying. It's like this is all a bad dream that won't end."

Dale began to speak, but Karen cut him off, raising her crutch. "But these things come in handy sometimes. Time to get moving." She turned away from him to wave at the audience to quiet down. Public speaking came easily to her, Dale thought. He rejoined his family.

"Ladies and gentlemen!" Karen proclaimed. "Welcome to the King George Polio Parade of Talent." She bowed to a round of applause. "We have many exceptional performances for you today. We will begin with our youngest patients, who are going to show off their progress!"

At that cue, she stepped aside. A few nurse's aides pushed four wheelchair-bound children, around six or seven years old, into the center of the hall. Charlene came forward on her crutches, while beside her, Mrs. Morris carried a wicker basket full of balls. Dale's heart leapt. Charlene's legs were strapped in braces around the ugly black shoes to keep her feet straight, but nevertheless, she was walking much more steadily than only a few weeks before. She wore a light blue blouse and a pleated dark blue skirt. Her hair was longer and brushed high into a ponytail.

Mrs. Morris set the basket down, and then fetched a chair for Charlene, putting it only a few feet from the children. Charlene handed the teacher her crutches and sat down, reached into the basket, and began to toss the balls carefully to the little ones, one at a time. Each catch was greeted with a "Bravo" and a "Look, she caught it!" from parents, delighted to see their children showing signs of recovery.

When that was done, the little kids bent over and pulled off their socks, which was met with surprised guffaws. Mrs. Morris set a small bowl and a row of ten marbles on the floor in front of each child. Dale took in a breath; he knew what they were going to do. This was one of the exercises he had found painful, but one he'd worked so hard at to get his feet moving again. His eyes fixed on the competitors' toes.

"On your marks," Charlene called out, "get set ... go!"

The children reached their legs forward, trying to pick up the marbles with their toes and deposit them in the bowls. They squealed and squirmed in their chairs, trying to grasp the glass beauties that rolled here and there. The audience cheered their successes, and groaned when the marbles rolled out of their reach. Dale's toes wriggled in sympathy.

"Stop!" Charlene declared and announced the winner—Diane, a six-year-old girl with a blonde pixie cut and two missing teeth. She'd managed to trap six marbles, while her closest competitor caught four. The little girl's pride was evident, and her parents teared up to see her so happy.

"That was so funny!" Brent declared.

Charlene's mother and father gave her a hug when she joined them on the side and took a seat to watch.

"Next," Karen declared, "the Polio Bunny Hop!" Ten kids came forward, jostling themselves into a line, those on crutches alternating with those in wheelchairs. From behind the crowd, someone put a needle on a record, and the brass band swelled.

The line started to sway, with the kids putting their right feet forward and their left feet out to the strains of the music. Some of them lifted their legs with their hands, or clumped them heavily on the footrests of their wheelchairs or on the floor.

When the song commanded, they all lifted their hands like bunny paws, and either bounced in their chairs as best as possible, or used their crutches to whap the floor.

The other kids broke out in gales of laughter and began to clap and cheer. Their parents, most of them a bit baffled, finally got the joke and joined in the laughter. As the song progressed, knees dipped and shoulders wiggled to the big band.

The conga line staggered forward, the upright kids pushing the wheelchairs, the kids in chairs reaching forward to hold the hips of those in front. Everyone joined in the singing.

A hearty applause congratulated the performers, some of whom were clearly tuckered out by their hijinks. Several parents squeezed their kids tightly when they rejoined the audience.

A new crew took over the center of the hallway, this time doing an eye and finger jive to "Shake, Rattle, and Roll." In unison, the kids lifted their hands in the air to the peal of the saxophones and Bill Haley's singing, flapping their wrists, bending their knuckles, and moving their eyes left, right, up, and down. The audience joined in—even Miss Clements, to Dale's surprise, singing and imitating the hand and eye movements. Brent hummed along beside Dale, moving his head from side to side. His father didn't participate, but when Dale snuck a glance at him, he could see the music relieving his tension.

Before the last verse, one of the boys exclaimed, "Okay, everyone, let's all do the Frog Gulp," and to the uproarious laughter from the patients and the embarrassment of the visitors, the performers all imitated iron lung patients, throwing their heads back to gasp for air, singing a few words, gasping again. By the end of the last chorus, they were all worn out, wheezing and panting. Dale peered over at Lindsay, who didn't seem to be paying attention to the joke a polio patient would appreciate the most. The audience responded with cheers and whistles. Dale realized he hadn't seen George; he made a mental note to visit him before he went home.

Karen brought the next act forward, a display of dexterity in bubble blowing skills. "You see how athletic we are?" she said, which drew more applause and laughter from the visitors and patients, when bubble gum was handed out all around. Nearly everyone's jaws worked away at the gum; bubbles snapping and gum sticking to faces prompted more laughter.

"Now, a special event," Karen announced, "with our own Dr. Barsky!" The crowd parted and Dr. Barsky walked forward haltingly, with a crutch under his right arm, his left leg dragging. His left arm hung loosely. Gasps and whispers filled the air.

He made it into the center of the hallway and swung his left arm up awkwardly, but people understood he wanted their attention.

"Hello, everyone," he said. "It's so nice to be back at King George. For those who don't know," he pivoted around to another part of the audience, "I am Dr. Percy Barsky, and I've had the pleasure of taking care of your children. I haven't been here for a few weeks, though, because unfortunately, I developed a mild case of polio myself." A buzz rippled through the crowd. He continued, "So I know how my patients feel, what they're going though."

An audience member called out the question they all wanted answered. "Were you in the hospital?"

"I was able to be treated at home, thankfully. And I'm going to be rid of this little helper in a week or two, I think," he replied, indicating his crutch. "I'll be one hundred percent, just a different kind of hundred percent." Several people began clapping, which grew into a round of warm applause.

He held up his arm again. "You're very kind, but the real champs are your children. I thought I understood what they were experiencing, but after contracting polio myself, I must tell you that I admire their courage and fight even more. It is a very tough fight." He bowed toward the children and continued, "Today, I want to show you the way one of our patients has developed special talents. Who knows? One day, he may be another kind of champion." He pivoted on the crutch again and called, "Morley, can I ask you to help, please?"

Morley advanced through the crowd, carrying an easel. A large white poster sat on the lip, a chess board outlined on it. Chess pieces drawn on big squares of paper were tacked in their places on the poster. Dr. Barsky led Morley toward the children in the iron lungs and stopped at Brent. Morley set the board up beside them so Brent could see it. Miss Nelson appeared out of nowhere. She had a double-faced chess clock, each side ready to track the amount of time the two players used in the game, and a small telephone table to set it on.

Dale and his father looked at each other, then moved back along the iron lung. Brent was blinking with excitement. Dale tried to find Charlene. Her parents were still where he'd seen them, but she had disappeared.

Dr. Barsky turned to the crowd. "As you know, not only do we help kids get better physically, we keep them up with their schoolwork. We also foster talents, and I'd like to show you an example of a talent we've discovered in one of our residents. I'd like to introduce Brent Melnyk." He smiled toward his young patient. "We're going to play a game of speed chess—a three-minute game, to show you that even if you have polio, you can accomplish a lot."

Miss Nelson set the timers and told Brent to begin. She pressed his clock. Brent knew what to do.

"Pawn to e4," he said. Morley took the tack out of the white pawn and moved it up two spaces. Miss Nelson clicked the timer to stop his clock and start Dr. Barsky's. Brent kept his eyes glued to the board.

Dr. Barsky countered. "Pawn to e5," and Morley obliged. Miss Nelson worked the clock.

"Knight to f3."

Dale felt a surge of pride for his little brother. The game went back and forth, with many visitors closing in around the competitors, and commenting on their moves and chances. There were lots of "Shhs" and "Quiet! They need to think," but Brent got the upper hand. With thirty seconds left, the crowd grew silent as the physician and the boy traded pieces and attacked. Miss Nelson's delicate clicks became quick bangs on the clock timer, as they began to shout their moves. Morley moved the pieces swiftly, barely keeping up.

"Rook takes e8. Check," Brent said. Dale heard a few spectators gasp.

With one second left on his clock, Dr. Barsky let out an "Oh, no!" and quickly moved his king up one square.

Brent still had eight seconds and it was his move.

"Queen to e7. Checkmate!" he shrieked, as loud as his voice would let him, then, "Yay!" and the crowd broke into applause.

Dale looked over the iron lung at his father, who was flushed, a tear running down his cheek. Amid the noise and excitement, he stepped forward and patted his son's head lovingly. Brent couldn't stop grinning. Dr. Barsky looked delighted.

"I'm really good, aren't I?" Brent bragged.

From the center of the hall, Karen whacked her crutch and called out, "Okay, now, for our last event today!" Several kids scurried or rolled as quickly as they could into the ward. One of them pushed in the record player on a wheeled cart and closed the door.

Dale thought Karen would explode, she looked so excited. "Without further ado," she said with a flourish, "Polio Beauties on Parade—Our Hospital Best!" She waved her hand toward the door, which opened to the music of Dean Martin's "That's Amore!"

Smiling kids slowly sashayed out of the ward, one by one. Each of them wiggled and swayed with the tune as much as they could, emphasizing the Italian word for "love"—*amore*, waving their arms in long swoops and acting sophisticated. Braces and crutches had been fancied up with ribbons. Models lumbered along on their own or were pushed from behind. The girls came first, dressed in their sleep finery, freshly ironed pajamas in flowers and stripes, fluffy chenille housecoats, and floppy slippers. A few of the girls preened like peacocks in silky, shiny kimonos with blossoms and lanterns in vibrant blues and reds. They'd rolled their hair into buns and decorated them with colorful barrettes. Dark curls tumbled down the back of another girl who adopted the haughtiness of a movie star in front of a camera. Her long, black and white checked robe was tied with a giant bow at the side, a long train flowing behind her that added to her air of mystery.

The music stopped and so did the catwalk. The models stood in place until "Sh-Boom" started up, so the boys could strut their stuff. A few of them had obviously borrowed their dads' formal housecoats, which were too wide and had huge lapels that encased them and made them look all grown up and hilarious. They sported pipes, pretending to inhale and blow out smoke rings. Karen hadn't convinced any of them to get crewcuts, Dale noted. Instead, most of them had slicked back, shiny hair, held in place by gobs of Brylcreem. Models and spectators all joined in on the chorus. Dale tapped his fingers on the side of Brent's iron lung. He saw his dad moving his head slightly to the music.

The crowd hooted and clapped as the last models flounced through. They pointed their noses in the air, and did their best to offer bored stares at the onlookers, but none of them could sustain their pretense. They all cracked up in smiles.

At a signal from Karen, the models all took their places in the middle of the aisle, half on each side, facing the center. Dale heard the scratching sound made by the needle on the record being picked up.

"And now," Karen said, bending at the waist and motioning toward the doorway of the ward. "A special announcement—" and Charlene walked into the hall.

She stood there, her arms extended, her fingers spread elegantly. Her crutches were balanced against her hips, showing off a flared turquoise skirt, with two yellow felt poodles prancing across the fabric. She wore a smart white blouse tucked into the skirt, and a blue hairband held her hair in place.

All the kids began to clap, and Dale could see Charlene's parents bursting with pride. She put her hands on the crutches again, and walked between the two rows of fashion models. She stopped in the middle, grinning from ear to ear. The models began to sing "My Best Girl." Dale thought she really did look gorgeous, all dressed up in her best Sunday clothes.

Karen took her place beside the singers and announced. "Ladies and gentlemen! We have a special announcement. Charlene Arcand is going home—today!"

The kids erupted in cheers; the parents clapped, some of them reaching over to cradle their children's heads or stroke their backs. Dale could see a few of them had tears in their eyes, happy for Charlene, wishing it were their child going home. Nurses and orderlies stood quietly; this was what they worked for, but they grew close to their patients, and missed them when they left.

Charlene stood in the middle, her hands pressing down on her crutches and her shoulders scrunched up. She seemed embarrassed to be the center of attention, but thrilled by it. Her parents stood back, their eyes fixed on their daughter.

"Can I go home soon, too, Dad?" Brent asked quietly,

no smile on his lips anymore. "Can I, please?"

"Soon," his father choked out. "Maybe soon."

Karen brought the show to a close. Everyone milled about in the hallway, making it difficult for Dale to break through the crowd. He needed to speak to Charlene.

"Excuse me," he said to one person, "pardon me," to another as he squeezed past.

By the time he got to Charlene, she was heading toward the stairs, waving at her friends. "I'll see you soon," she called out. "Yes, I will come back. Bye!" She gave her father her crutch and reached for the bannister. She saw Dale. "Oh," she said, her smile vanishing.

Dale stood there, now unable to speak. Her father turned to him. "Are you the boy who was looking for our house last week?"

Embarrassed, Dale squeaked out, "Uh ... yes." Charlene screwed up her eyes, looking puzzled.

"Hmph ... my cousin told me." He returned to Charlene. "Let's go, my girl," he said, and took her crutches. Her mother took her arm and guided Charlene carefully down, shielding her as others brushed by. Charlene turned back once to look briefly at Dale, but showed no expression.

The crowd of parents and grandparents was thinning out now, many of them returning to the wards with the kids. The mood was upbeat, compared to the gloom that enveloped Dale.

"She really liked you." Karen was suddenly beside him. Dale started. He hadn't seen her approach.

"I'm so stupid," Dale muttered. Off in the corner, he saw Morley push Lindsay's bed back to the ward.

"Hey," he said to her. "I meant to ask you before. Where's George? Why didn't you have a wheelchair race?"

Karen's face reddened. She swallowed, took in a deep breath, and slowly hobbled away.

"He died a few days ago."

Dale whirled around to see Miss Nelson. "I'm sorry, Dale," she said, her voice wobbling "He wasn't the success story we'd hoped for. His lungs finally gave out. There was nothing anyone could do." Her eyes became misty. "I'm sorry." She took Dale's arm. "I'm so glad you're better, though."

Peter was waiting on the other side of the hallway. He wheeled up as Miss Nelson left. "Charlene told Karen she would do the announcing today, but Karen insisted. That was hard for her to do. But guess what?

Lindsay took it hard, too. He told me he wished it had been him, that George was too good a guy." He shook his head. "Crazy thing is, Lindsay hasn't been making stupid remarks. I guess he realizes that if he's alive, that he'd better stop sneering or he won't have any friends."

Dale put his hand out on the bannister for support.

"I know this is tough news. We're pretty torn up about it, too," Peter said. "Listen, Dale, you take care, okay?" He slowly wheeled away.

CHAPTER 19

The streetcar ride home took forever, Dale's father silent as usual. They stepped down into the late Sunday afternoon heat at the top of Smithfield Avenue, across from the Roco.

"Some nice fellows in that shop," Dad said, nodding toward the garage as they walked past it. "And I really enjoy the tinkering on the engines. Every one is a new challenge. It makes me feel good to see people smile when their engines hum," he said. "They trust my work." He nodded to himself in approval.

Dale said nothing, only looked up at the leaves rustling on the elm trees. A few neighbors were out in the yard.

"Afternoon!" Mr. Malchy called out as he raked his lawn. Dale could see Mr. Malchy glancing across the grass at his legs, probably wondering how Dale had been affected by polio. Across the street, Mr. Glass waved, but neither of them asked his dad and him to stop and chat. Dale understood how the Palmer family felt when they sat alone in their front yard, victims for life of both polio and fear.

Opening the door to the summer porch, his father cleared his throat. "Well, that was a good day, wasn't it? Guess it's lucky I got the job so close to home, eh," he said jauntily. He lifted one of the windows and fresh air seeped through the screen. "That's better." He moved to lift the rest of them.

Dale couldn't believe what he had heard. "What was so good about today, Dad?" he said, slamming the door. "And what's all that talk about it being so great to work at Roco? You might as well work at the railway, or even a million miles away." His boldness frightened him.

"What do you mean?" His father stopped opening windows.

Dale spat out his words. "You don't care about us. You don't care that I was sick; you just want me to work all the time. You don't care that I want to play hockey, that I might have some ambition." He breathed in and out. "You don't care that it's *your fault* that Brent is sick, maybe never going to get out of that stupid iron lung.

He's a little kid! Did you ask him if he had a good day? For him, every day is the same now." Dale felt the heat rise in his face. The air in the confined porch was still hot and steamy. "He's a little kid, and now he's paralyzed—because you didn't listen!"

His father looked stricken. "That's not true ... I didn't believe it. I wasn't sure—"

"You didn't believe—what? Who cares what you *believed*? What does what you believe have to do with facts? How about listening to people who made the vaccine to save kids from exactly what Brent has? How about that?" He could feel his heart pounding.

"But—"

"But what?" Dale said, his words pouring out. "You believe some guy on the radio who talks fast and knows a lot about movie stars? How does he know more than a doctor?" He couldn't believe he was talking this way to his father.

"I don't trust doctors," his father fired back, lifting his head and waving his arm. "We never went to a doctor when I was a kid. They charged money. For what—a little cough medicine? They're crooks!" He wagged his index finger to prove the point.

"Trust! You brag about how customers trust you to make their cars safe and keep them alive. You're proud you know what you're doing. So why did you decide doctors can't be trusted to keep us healthy—and alive? Why do you trust Dr. Barsky to help Brent? Is he a crook? Do you want to explain that logic?" Dale took another breath. "That story about your grandfather had nothing to do with money. Did you ever think that maybe he was too far gone when the doctors finally operated. And you're lucky you never got really sick, that's all. I'm sick of hearing you tell us that everything will be fine only because *you* were lucky. Brent wasn't lucky—he's paralyzed—because of you! Paralyzed! It didn't have to happen."

Then he said what he'd wanted to say for a long time. He pointed his finger at his father. "Mom's heart failed, but you wouldn't let her go to the doctor when she started to get weak all the time, because you think you know more than a doctor! What makes you such an expert?"

"I didn't know," his father said, gritting his teeth, still holding his arm crooked in the air.

"That's right," Dale said, dropping his voice. "You didn't know, so you decided for her, instead of asking someone who might know. What do you think they studied medicine for?"

"They said she might have died anyway." That came out in a whisper. His dad dropped his arm and slid his hand in his pants pocket. He leaned against the window frame.

"But what if they could have saved her?" Dale cried, throwing his hand up. He couldn't stop. "They would have tried! You didn't even let her check. You told her she would be fine, that she was being dramatic when she said she needed to rest. Then it was too late! Now I don't have a mom—Brent is a little kid, and he doesn't have a mom, and he needs one!" He could feel the sweat beading under his hairline. "You're a terrible father. You don't care about us, just about saving money. Now Mom's dead—and Brent has polio, because you're proud of your stupidity. And you're mean!"

His chest heaved. He wanted to throw up. He collapsed on the old sofa behind him, tears rolling down his face.

A breeze picked up, making the leaves on the trees rustle. The father and son didn't move. His dad's breathing was shallow, his eyes locked in place.

After a long time, Dad said, "I loved your mother, too. I miss her." He sank into a wicker chair behind him.

"Yes," Dale said slowly, flicking a piece of dust on the couch. "But she's dead. And Brent is paralyzed."

He bolted from the sofa and out of the porch. When he got to the sidewalk, he shoved his hands hard into his pockets and locked his elbows, to keep from waving his arms around as he criticized and cursed his father. He pounded his heels into the concrete, driving himself forward with anger. He kicked the curbs when he recalled his father's faults, denting the toe of his shoe.

He walked for hours in the heat, up one street and down another. He went in the opposite direction of the community center, not the least bit interested in meeting anyone associated with hockey. He needed to be alone.

Sweat soaked his clothes. It was nearly suppertime before he dragged himself back to Smithfield Avenue. He had reviewed all his father's arrogance and ignorance, all of his attitudes and indifference to his wife and sons. His father's pride had been misplaced, with terrible consequences. He decided he would never act that way if he had a family.

But he couldn't help but also remember the warm moments before his mom died, when they'd laughed together at dinner, gone for family walks, played catch in the park. Dad used to cheer his hockey triumphs as loudly as every other parent. His mother would have wanted Dale to forgive him. So would Brent. He and Brent needed to be cared for, and Dad needed caring for, too.

When he opened the door to the porch, he was stunned to see his father still sitting in the wicker chair. His tie and collar were undone, his hair disheveled. His face was pale. Most of the windows were still shut. The heat was stifling.

"Dad," Dale said, "are you all right?" He shut the door.

After another long pause, his father raised his eyes and looked at his son. "I'm sorry," he whispered, "I'm sorry."

The breeze swirled through the few windows they had opened earlier. Dale reached his hand out and pulled his father up. Together, they staggered into the house to recover.

CHAPTER 20

"You see what happens when you do what I tell you?" Beaming, Mrs. Stewart stood back, her hands on her hips. "You're better!" Across the therapy room, children pulled themselves along the parallel bars, flopping onto the mattress when their arms gave out. Over in the pool, a girl shouted at the attendant stretching her legs.

"Do you think I am?" Dale asked, looking down at his legs. It seemed like it was yesterday that he'd been a patient in the hospital, wearing heavy braces strapped on each leg, when each step felt like a lunge. Now, only a few months later, he could walk confidently for long distances, and run lightly for a short time. His breath and stamina had returned. The summer had been a rebirth for him.

Still, he needed reassurance. "But will I be able to skate? Will I be as quick?" He grimaced. "Will I be able to make the starter position?"

"You're doing what I told you to do, aren't you?" Mrs. Stewart said. "Those exercises I added a few weeks ago are making a difference, lad. I can't promise you anything. But you're alive; you got out of an iron lung—think about what you've been through!" She ticked off his achievements on her fingers. "Not many people who were as sick as you have recovered so well."

"I guess I shouldn't complain, should I?"

"No, you shouldn't, my boy. I think even crabby Miss Clements would be pleased for ya." Mrs. Stewart raised an eyebrow.

"You think so? I haven't seen her when I've come for treatments."

"Tha's because she's no longer in the employ of the hospital, shall we say." Mrs. Stewart tapped her chin in a knowing way.

"She quit?"

"Let's say she agreed she should look elsewhere for work," Mrs. Stewart said, shaking her head. "Ach, you shouldn't be a nurse if you don't like children."

"You mean 'bairns,'" Dale kidded.

Mrs. Stewart laughed. "I've taught you more than a few physical exercises, I see," she said. Then, with a hearty handshake and a wagging finger as a reminder to keep on exercising, she discharged Dale from her program.

He also made sure to take a few minutes each day to practice darting his eyes back and forth, imagining pucks coming from all sides. It was a little more difficult to practice his hockey skills alone, but he bought a rubber ball with his allowance, and smacked it against the side of the house, then caught it on the rebound, over and over. He wrote in his diary about what he had experienced.

If you had said this would happen to me, I wouldn't have believed it. And when I was sick, I expected I would be sick forever, but I'm not. I'm getting stronger every day. Who knows? Maybe I'll be the first NHL goalie to have recovered from polio. From iron lung to the Stanley Cup—what a story!

I hear Paul has gone to live with his grandparents. I wish he had come around, but maybe I should have knocked on his door. We had a good time together. I miss him.

He'd done a lot of work around the house with his father, who was as good at handiwork as he was at fixing cars. They began to talk as they worked, and the more they did, the nightmares that haunted Dale faded away.

While they were scraping the chipped paint off the front of the house, Dale told Dad how his heart broke when his mother died, and his dad told him the story of how they'd met.

He'd signed up with the Royal Canadian Air Force during World War II, and was posted at a base not far from Winnipeg, assigned as an instructor for wireless operators.

"We had a Saturday night off," he said. "A buddy and I saw a poster for a dance. On a whim, we caught a lift into the city, and went to see what it was like. That's where I saw Grace," he said quietly. "The band began to play 'Charmaine.'" He stood back from his work and smiled at Dale. "I walked across the room and asked her to dance. She made me laugh right away. That was it for me. I was smitten." His smile grew wider.

Dad scraped a few more chips. "We fell in love and got married pretty quickly," he continued. "I wasn't sent overseas—the Air Force kept me here as an instructor." He grinned, and Dale could see Brent's face in his. "That was the best whim I ever followed."

"Dad," Dale exclaimed, "you're a romantic guy!"

"I could be." Dad's voice fell again. "I was." He stopped speaking and pushed the scraper hard against the wood.

A few days later, Dale got up the nerve to broach the topic of girls he might consider liking. He told his dad what Mom had said about dating people of different religions, and then confessed what had happened with Charlene.

"Oh, that," his father said. They were making the best of the summer evening to finish working on the front of the house. "Your mother was a wonderful woman, but she wasn't perfect. We had a lot in common, and she had a good heart, a good sense of humor, all the things I needed. But I'll be honest with you. I don't know what would have happened if we had been different religions, or different colors. I would like to think I would have followed my heart and said those things didn't matter."

His dad seemed to be surveying their paint strokes, then said firmly, "I would like to think that if anybody told me I couldn't go out with Grace, I would have fought for her, no matter what!" He dipped his brush in the paint tray and spread it on the board.

Dale shrugged his shoulders, at a loss for important words. "But lots of people say—"

"I know what people say. And I know that those people judge me for the way I treated your mother, and you, and Brent." Dad added paint to the board below. "But I know what's important now, and it isn't a person's religion or the color of their skin. Is she a good person? A good friend? Funny? Smart? That's what's important. Think about that, not what people say."

"You mean, you wouldn't care if I liked Charlene?" Dale asked.

Dad kneeled to work on the lowest boards. He looked up at Dale. "I know if you asked your grandmother, she'd have trouble with it, and you'd have to be tough enough to deal with guff from a lot of other people. But who's supposed to be happy—Grandma, them, me, or you?" He laid his brush on the paint tray and straightened up. "So tell me. Is she nice?" he asked.

The question caught Dale off guard. "Yes," he declared. "Yes, she's terrific!"

"Is she smart? Funny?"

"Yes!" Dale gushed, embarrassed.

"Well," Dad said, "what else really matters?" He picked

up the tray and heaved a big sigh, turning to look Dale in the eye. "I made a lot of mistakes with you boys," he said slowly. "It shows you how important your mother was. I didn't know what to do or how to act without her common sense." He clicked his tongue. "I will try to do better, I promise." He nodded, then said, "I'm going to clean up."

Dad walked away to the back yard. Dale could feel the resentment he had developed toward his father lifting.

He stood quietly for a few moments. "Charlene ... Charmaine," he said to himself, pleased at the pleasant sounds. He gazed down the street, wishing she would appear.

Mr. Winocur had helped them with their household renovations, when he learned Brent would be returning home in the coming weeks. Brent's paralysis had not gone away.

"The term is 'tetraplegic,'" Dr. Barsky told them. "All his limbs are affected as well as his breathing."

Dad had been crestfallen at the news. "I guess I held out hope," he said.

"He's growing, so his breathing muscles might get stronger," Dr. Barsky said. "Which means, he may be able to get out of the machine for some hours during the day." He told them the hospital thought Brent could live safely at home in the iron lung, with trained assistants organized to care for him.

"Remember that his mind is healthy and strong," Dr. Barsky said. "Feed his intellect. He may do great things, only in a different way."

Dad spent a few days not saying much, standing around, gazing at nothing. Dale knew he would always feel a sense of guilt for refusing to have Brent vaccinated.

Then he began work on the house, and on his determination to be a better father. Mr. Winocur helped them remove the front wall of the bedroom, so Brent could be included in the goings-on in the household, and Dale constructed a folding wooden divider on wheels, that could be rolled in easily to give him privacy when he wanted it.

Grandma offered to help, too, which she said would help her deal with losing her daughter. She planned on surprising Brent with two goldfish in a glass bowl, so he could watch them swim around in their little world. Mrs. Morris had been hired as a traveling teacher for children learning at home, like Brent.

Whenever he'd had a physiotherapy session, Dale had gone down to the children's ward and spent an hour or two with Brent. The hospital library had received donations of more books, so there was a greater selection to read aloud to Brent. At first, Dale read light-hearted stories to make Brent laugh, but after a few of those, Brent had asked for more serious stories.

"I like to think about things," he told Dale. "I have a lot of time to think now. I like adventure, too. Can you find me books like that?"

"Your wish is my command," Dale said, and on the next visit, he began reading him *Treasure Island*, plunging into the world of Jim Hawkins and Long John Silver.

Brent confided he'd always wanted to be a pirate, to captain a ship and search for buried gold. "It sounds really dangerous," he said, "and so much fun. Maybe I'll be one, some day!"

"Maybe," Dale said, running his hand through his brother's hair. "You never know."

Dr. Barsky returned to work without his crutch, but he still had a weak left arm, and now he walked with a slight limp. His cheery attitude, though, never wavered. "Other people have it worse," he said to Dad.

"I can still make a living, be a good husband and dad, so I'm not complaining." They had met at Brent's bedside to tell him about their plans to welcome him home. "And—I can still play chess with you, if you like, Brent. Do I have your permission to come over and play sometimes?"

"Yes!" Brent blurted, then asked, "I mean ... can he, Dad?"

Dad laughed. "Yes, for sure," he said. "Maybe you can teach me to play, too. I'm all thumbs when it comes to chess."

"If you like, I'll sign you up with a group that plays postal chess," Dr. Barsky offered. "You mail a single move to an opponent on a postcard, then wait for their reply. The game can take a few weeks or even a few months to complete, but if you have several opponents, you can learn a lot about different styles of play."

Brent looked at his dad. "Can I do that, Dad?"

"What a good idea!" Dad said. "We can help you with that, Brent. Dale or I can mail the postcards whenever you like." Then he cleared his throat and announced, "We're also going to get a television. I've got to save, so it won't be right away—"

Brent interrupted. "A television! Really? Didn't you want to save for a car, Dad? A green one?""

"I do want a car," Dad said, "but we can get by for now. If you can't go to the movies like other children, you can watch science shows or hockey games, so you know what's going on. Your friends can come over. I've already spoken with their mothers." He cleared his throat again and looked at Dale. "We can all watch it together."

Brent jabbered on about how they could watch the hockey stars making their great plays. Dale could see thoughts of future possibilities whirling through his head.

"Thanks, Dad," Dale said. "Thanks."

"I think the house needs a little brightening up, too," Dad said. "What do you think about getting a budgie to chirp and keep you company, Brent?"

"Wow!" Brent hooted. "Yes, please! I can teach it to talk, right? What color?"

"Yellow," said Dale. "Right, Dad?"

His father nodded. "Good idea."

"I can cook now," Dale told Brent. "No more peanut butter sandwiches for supper."

"Whew," Brent said and looked at their father. "Those were really boring. Sorry, Dad," he said.

"No offense taken. They really were boring," Dad admitted. "Your brother has made supper a meal I look forward to."

Dale returned to school in September, and after some initial uncertainty, the kids stopped being afraid of associating with him. As with Paul, many of their parents had given them instructions to stay far away from him. Then Halloween came, and with it, snow and the freeze-up. Dale helped hose down the surface at the community center, layering the sheets of freezing water to make them smooth. A week later, hockey season began. Life and his relationships were getting back to normal.

Dale heard that Paul had easily won the coveted starter position on the Northwood team. The tryouts at Perth, though, were no cakewalk. New kids had moved into the neighborhood during the summer, and a few of them were strong, skilled competitors.

CHAPTER 21

Mr. Leah stood back. "Stand up straight," he ordered.

Dale drew himself up on his skates, squared his shoulders, and inhaled deeply. He banged his goalie stick aggressively on the cement floor. He always waited until a game was over, before inscribing the details on the shaft. "How do I look?" he asked his coach.

Mr. Leah chortled. "Well, you still have a toothy grin, which is nice, isn't it?" He nodded. "You look good, Dale."

Today was the first game of the season.

Old teammates and new, they were all eager to play, thumping each other's shoulders, shifting their shoulder pads. Their uniforms were as moth-eaten as always. Dale stuck his nose in his goalie jersey, inhaling the odor of the naphtha balls. How good it smelled to him! He thought of his mother, as he pulled the jersey over his head. He stood in front of the dressing room mirror, examining the new holes that joined those she had stitched only a year before. He took a moment to remember her with gratitude. He'd grown, so the jersey rode a little higher on his waist. She would have been pleased to see how tall and strong he was becoming, to see that one pair of warm socks was enough for his skates to fit this season; his feet were a full size larger. He lined up with the rest of the team to get on the ice, and began doing some last-minute eye exercises before they trooped out.

Suddenly, his stomach cramped and rebelled. It caught him off guard—he'd never been nervous to play before. He tightened his stomach muscles to fend off the strange sensation, kept his eyes focused on the back of the player in front of him, hoping no one saw his discomfort, hoping that it had nothing to do with polio. He had a panicked thought about it returning to claim him, the way it had claimed George. He breathed slowly and deeply, in and out ... in and out ... in and out. By the time the line moved out, the waves of nausea had eased.

He hit the ice to the cheers of the spectators leaning over the boards. Their welcome made him realize how much he had missed the fight to control the puck, the joy of the game.

Dad was there, clapping his gloves together, when Dale took his position on the bench as the backup goalie. Grandma had come to spend the afternoon with Brent, who vowed he would teach his grandmother to play chess.

Then Northwood took to the ice. Dale decided to chalk his stomach rumbles up to worrying about seeing Paul as a true opponent for the first time. Northwood fans were there in force, too. Out of the corner of his eye, Dale saw his father walk over to Paul's dad. The two men hadn't seen each other since their sons parted ways. They shook hands, and leaned on the boards together, chatting.

Paul was last out on the ice. He skated to the middle of the rink, then turned and skated to the Perth bench. "Hi Dale," Paul stammered. "I ... uh ..."

Dale reached over the board and slapped Paul's glove with his own. "Good luck," he said.

Paul smiled quickly. "You, too." He slapped Dale's glove in return. Paul glided over to take his place in the Northwood net.

The game was fast and fun. Both teams were en-thusiastic and strong. The new players skated well, and popped the puck past Paul six times during the game, although he kept out many more with his crouched butter-fly stance. Dale saw Paul make saves in ways he'd never done before. He had grown over the summer, too, and he showed a greater presence in the crease. The new goalie on the Perth team was nimble; he also used the butterfly stance, and displayed lightning quick reflexes. From his spot on the bench, Dale could see him tracking the puck, calculating ahead where it would be shot.

"He's good, isn't he?" one of the rookies commented, as he waited for his turn on the ice. Dale saw the newbie twitch and flinch as he followed the action.

"Better than good," Dale admitted. "He's going to be fantastic."

The game was over before he realized it. The combination of experience and new energy on the Perth team proved to be a winning combination over Northwood. The new goalie played consistently through all three periods, letting in four goals, also saving more than Dale could count. The fans—mostly brothers, sisters, and school friends—jumped up and down.

Dale saw his dad stamping his feet to ward off the cold. He smiled at Dale, not displaying any concern that his son hadn't had any ice time. When the final whistle blew, the team erupted in delight. Dale felt a thrill, almost as if he had helped snag their first victory of the season. He laughed and cheered with the rest of the players. His teammates swarmed the new goalie, as they headed into the dressing room.

Paul skated over to the Perth box. He was breathing hard, his cheeks were flaming red with the cold, and his nose was running. Still, he was smiling from ear to ear. He started to speak when Dale interrupted. "You're the next Terry Sawchuk," he said. Paul's eyes widened.

"We lost, but I felt good out there," he wheezed, rubbing his nose on the sleeve of his jersey. "Too bad you didn't get to play."

"That's okay," Dale assured him. "The way I felt today, I was more like Glenn Hall, anyway. Hey," he punched his friend's arm, "you're going to be a star for Northwood—maybe Paul Alexander will be an NHL star!"

Paul punched him back.

"Sorry about everything that happened," Paul said. "I didn't mean the things I said."

From the other side of the rink, Paul's teammates called out for him to join them.

He held up his big gloved hand. "Coming." Turning

back to Dale, he said, "Let's get together, sometime soon."

Quickly, the two boys arranged to see each other in the coming days.

"Great game, boys," Mr. Leah called over the din. "I'm proud of you. You played like a team!" The coach's cheeks were red, his eyes watering from the cold, his glasses fogged with condensation. He took a handkerchief out of his pocket and wiped the moisture off the lenses. "Get dressed and I'll be back in a minute for a short talk. Today's a day to celebrate." He went down the hall toward his office.

Dale eased himself out of his skates and rubbed his chilled toes, bending them slowly to restore the warmth, proud that he could bend them. Other boys were gloating, thrilled with their win. The first-time players were now firmly part of their team.

He searched through his coat pocket to find the pencil he'd brought, and inscribed the game date and the win on the shaft of his stick. After changing out of his hockey pants and skates, he went to find Mr. Leah.

"Dale! Wasn't that something? What a game!" Mr. Leah was at his tiny desk in his office, scribbling notes on a pad of paper. He motioned to the chair opposite him. "Sit down, please. I know I didn't use you, but I wanted to test—"

"He was great," Dale said, settling on the chair. "I'm glad you left him in. But I wanted to tell you that … I'm not going to play hockey this year—not league hockey, anyway. I'm just going to play pick-up games when I can." He felt strangely relieved to say it. "You can give my spot to one of the new kids—I'm giving up my position."

Mr. Leah sat up and gestured. "What? Don't be sore, Dale. You'll get to play—"

Dale shook his head. "No, no, I'm not mad. It's okay. I don't want it anymore. Really."

Mr. Leah leaned one elbow on the table. "Are you sure? Why, Dale? You might be back in the starting position soon, and with the two of you, I think we can win the championship this year. And what about getting to the NHL? You could do it. You probably need a little more time to get stronger."

"That's okay," Dale said, stretching out his legs. "It's not that important for me anymore. I want to help my dad take care of Brent. It's more important to me than playing, than making the NHL."

"But you love hockey. You have talent," Mr. Leah urged.

"Thanks," Dale said. "Yeah, I do love hockey, which is why I want to know if I can help you coach, so I can still be part of the team." He reached into his back pocket, pulled out his diary, and flipped it open to show Mr. Leah pages full of writing and diagrams. "I write about how I play," he said. "I analyze my moves in words, then I sketch it out. I used it as part of my own training program. I think I got better because I took each move apart. I used these ideas to coach Brent, too, so maybe I could help you with coaching kids who need extra attention."

Mr. Leah straightened the glasses on his nose, flipping the pages back and forth. He looked up at Dale. "You did this?" he asked. "You never told me."

Dale shrugged. "Well, you make notes, so I thought it would help me, too. I did it at home, after games."

"Hmm, this is something," the coach said. He went through the book again. He drew it closer to his eyes, then drew his thumb down rough edges in the center of the book. "You've taken out some pages," he said.

"Personal stuff," Dale said. "I've put them in another

scribbler, for my eyes only. I've had a lot on my mind."

"Well, you've been through a lot this year. Writing about it is probably a good way to work through it," Mr. Leah said. He crossed his legs and rested the open diary on his knee.

One of the other players appeared in the doorway. "We're all dressed, Mr. Leah," he said, puzzled at seeing Dale in the office.

"I'll be right there," Mr. Leah said. "Dale, wait here, all right?" He put the diary on the desk.

Mr. Leah returned a few minutes later. "I gave them the pat on the back they deserved. Now," he said, an excited tone in his voice, returning to the diary and adjusting his glasses again. "How about you and I have a talk about how you can help me, and how I can help you."

"How can you help me?" Dale asked. "I'm only going to play pickup games on the rink near my house, so I can be home more with Brent."

"Well, I'd be happy to have you as an assistant coach on the team, but how about I also pay you to write about hockey?" Mr. Leah asked, looking over the top of his glasses.

"Pay me? Pay me money? What would I have to do?"

Mr. Leah had his attention. He took a deep breath.

"Yes, I'll pay you money." Mr. Leah laughed again, slapping Dale's knee. "Real money. You know what I do for a living, don't you, Dale?"

"You write about sports in the Tribune. I know that."

The newspaperman leaned toward Dale. "I'm the editor of the sports department," he said. "That's why my name is at the top of the first page of that section. I decide who writes about sports for the paper."

Goosebumps burst out on Dale's arms. The realization of what that meant grew on him. "You want me to write for the Tribune?" He sat up in his chair. "Really?"

"I think you might be able to," Mr. Leah said, turning the pages. "You've got an ability to analyze sports. Fans like that." He took off his glasses and put them on the desk. "But I'm going to tell you another reason why I'm so interested in your success, Dale, whether you want to fill up the net or fill up a piece of paper. I had polio, too, you know, when I was a little kid."

"You did?" Dale's voice rose and his eyes were immediately drawn to Mr. Leah's leg. He'd never seen him limp or favor his legs at all.

Mr. Leah nodded slowly. "It was a terrible time. It

was 1921, and I was only eight years old. Luckily, my lungs weren't affected, because there weren't any iron lungs then—they weren't invented until 1928, so a lot of children died in those days. There were no special hospitals, no one knew how to treat it." He waited another moment before he continued. "But I recovered, and I've had the opportunity to do what I love best—write about sports and coach kids to be the best they can be."

He settled back on his chair and feathered the pages of Dale's diary with his thumb. "So, if you don't want to be a goalie, what about writing about sports? Here's my proposal: I can see you understand the structure of the plays." He took off his glasses. "Why don't you write me a short article about hockey plays every few weeks— best moves for defensemen, forwards, goalies—you know what I mean. We can tailor it to mention certain players and their styles, give examples of important plays, and we can include them as sidebars when we write about big games."

Dale was stunned. "How do I start?" he stuttered.

"Why don't you write a sample article, maybe comparing the stand-up goalie method to the butterfly style—maybe compare Terry Sawchuk to Glenn Hall.

Local readers would love that, wouldn't they? Show me a draft, and I'll help you craft it for the newspaper. An editor is a coach, after all." He smiled and put his glasses back on his nose.

Dale's head swam with what he had heard.

Mr. Leah tapped the diary again. "We have one thing left to discuss," he said. "How does $1 per short article sound? Double that if you get up to longer pieces."

"A dollar? Maybe $2? Sure!" Dale sprang from his chair. "Uh ... thanks, Mr. Leah," he stumbled, and pumped the coach's hand far too hard, then stopped in mid-pump. "But—can I ask you a favor?"

"Go ahead. What is it?"

Dale ran his hand down the ratty jersey his mother had desperately tried to mend. "This. My mom fixed it and I'd like to have it." He breathed in deeply, then exhaled and asked, "Can I buy it from the team?"

Mr. Leah stood up and smiled. "Buy it?" He clapped Dale on the shoulder. "What would I charge you for— all those holes?" He chuckled. "Take it, and think of your mom when you look at it. Throw a naphtha ball in the drawer when you put it away, though, or soon there really will be nothing left." He pointed to the hallway.

"Now, go—your dad is waiting in the locker room. Tell him about our plans. See you soon."

"Thanks!" Dale ran out the door to tell his father his news—and that he could help contribute to the purchase of the television.

CHAPTER 22

The steps on the St. John's library had been cleared of the snow that had fallen overnight. Dale pulled on the heavy wooden door, stepped into the foyer, and stamped his boots clean. The dark wood in the old building gleamed, even on the stairs leading down to the children's collection.

He headed down, depositing the books he'd taken out a week earlier on the librarian's desk. Brent had asked for a few favorite stories, and Dale had in mind to take out a book on chess instruction, so he could learn some basic strategies and Brent could learn new moves.

He pulled out the "C" drawer on the library catalogue and thumbed the cards until he came to "ch" and "chess." The Dewey Decimal number was 794. Using the small pencils provided on the top of the card catalogue, he wrote down the location of a few books and went off looking for the right shelf.

He turned the corner to the 700s and stopped. Charlene's head was tilted to the left as she read titles printed on the spines. She shifted her hand crutch and pulled out a book, set it in the space at the end of the shelf, and opened it up to examine it.

"Hi," Dale squeaked out.

She looked up and made an "O" shape with her mouth, then responded. "Hi!"

Dale didn't know how to proceed, but his father's words had jangled in his head since they had talked. "How—how are you?" he asked. "Do you live around here now? I thought—"

"We moved," Charlene said. Her hair had grown longer since Dale had last seen her. She looked perfect in her blue wool coat and the white handknit scarf wrapped around her neck. She wore big galoshes, which he assumed hid those black shoes they all hated, and the braces that fit into those shoes; he could see she needed them and the crutches. "We rented a house down the street. It's a long story," she said, clicking her tongue.

"Oh! So you go to school right across the street?" Dale said.

"Yeah, St. John's High."

"How is it? Do you like it?" He searched for something positive to say, knowing how unhappy she had been.

She screwed up her mouth and waggled her head. "I guess it's okay. I've got new friends." She raised an eyebrow. "Of course, a few idiots make fun of me because I have crutches, or because I'm not like them," she said. "But I guess that's going to be my life." She shrugged.

He took a quiet breath and decided to pursue a different topic. "What kind of books are you looking for?" he asked.

"Drawing books for my little sisters," Charlene said. Three young girls, one about ten years old, the second about eight, and the third a little younger, all looking like Charlene, ran up with armloads of books. They giggled when they saw Dale talking to their big sister. Charlene gave them the books she was holding, and tried to shoo them away, but her efforts only made them titter and squeal to each other.

"Keep the noise down, you brats. Get away," Charlene chided, but she was laughing. Finally, she exiled them to a nearby table where they pretended to read, all the while peeking back at Charlene as often as possible.

"Did any of them get polio?" Dale asked.

"Nope," Charlene said. "My parents made sure they were vaccinated as soon as they could. They didn't want them to suffer the way I did."

Dale exhaled, thinking about how Brent's fate had been different.

They exchanged information right there in the aisle, leaning against the shelves—about Karen, who had gone home, still grieving George's death. "She cried a lot," Charlene remembered quietly. "She said she really loved him, that she knows she'll never love anyone else. But now that she's away from the hospital, she'll be able to look ahead. I'm pretty sure about that," she said, and added, "I know it worked for me."

"What do you mean?" Dale asked.

She shrugged. "I do my exercises—every day." She breathed out heavily. "But I'm never going to get much better. I'll always need these things." She motioned to her braces and crutches. "So, I thought, well, I won't be able to be a nurse. I was upset, because that's what I always wanted to be. I told Morley before I was discharged. You should have seen how mad he got at me!" She grinned at the recollection. "The next day, he came back to the hospital with a woman—it was his Aunt Katie. She has braces and crutches, like I do—and guess what: she's a nurse." Charlene's smile lit up her face.

"She came here from Holland, after World War II. She told me that when the Nazis invaded her country, they confiscated all the crops and animals from farms to feed their army. People were starving, so they dug up tulip bulbs or ate grass to stay alive. The bones in her legs became brittle because of malnutrition, so she's got to support her body with the braces and crutches. But she wanted to be a nurse, and she also wanted to leave Holland—to get away from what happened there. She had relatives in Canada, so she came." Charlene smiled. "She did what she said she would. She works in an old folks' home now, and she says she's very happy."

"Wow," Dale said. "That's something."

"Yes, it is," Charlene said, pursing her lips. "So, if she can do it, so can I. Mrs. Stewart told me stories about how she helped injured soldiers, how her work made a difference to them, and how much they appreciated it. That made me even more interested." Then she imitated a Scottish accent. "She told me, 'Of course you can be a nurse, lassie. It's what's in your head and your heart, not only your legs.'"

She looked up at Dale and flashed her pretty smile. "And guess what else she said?"

"What?"

"She told me her daughter is 'grown up and doing fine,' and that she'd be glad to help me study to get into nursing."

"What?" Dale exclaimed.

"Yeah, she told my parents, too. She said, 'Smart people should have opportunities, and your lass is a smart girl,' and she gave them her address to keep in touch. My parents think she's terrific."

"Wow, that's so nice!"

Charlene smiled even more. "Is it ever! Good old Mrs. Stewart, eh? And we made fun of her all the time! She gave me a second chance, didn't she? She wouldn't let me alone. I feel so guilty, but I guess she knew we liked her." Charlene clucked her tongue. "I'm babysitting whenever I can to save for nursing school, and I've been thinking about the kinds of jobs I might do when I'm sixteen, like work at the cash register in a drug store. My mom and dad will do whatever they can, too." She jutted her chin in her sisters' direction. "Maybe that will make them think about what they want to do when they grow up." She shifted her weight on her leg. "I want to do it, so I stopped feeling sorry for myself. I'm going to show people who thought I couldn't accomplish anything. There is another chance for me, and I think there will be one for Karen."

The tension between them seemed to have melted away. They talked for a few minutes more, with Charlene's sisters interrupting as much as they could. She sent them on a mission to get more stories.

Miss Clements, Charlene thought, had been forced to quit or had been fired. "I felt a little sorry for her. But it was her fault. All she had to do was be polite. It was like she was mad at us for having polio, like we did something wrong." She lifted an eyebrow. "And guess who suddenly tried to be friendly to me," she said.

"Who?"

"Lindsay." Dale's eyes widened in surprise. "He called me over to his bed the morning of the talent show, right before I was discharged. I didn't want to go over, but he asked me again. So I did. He said, 'Listen, I want to wish you good luck.' Then he shut his eyes tight."

"He said that? Nothing else?"

"That was it," she said. "He didn't make fun of me or

say anything nasty. You could tell it was really hard for him to be nice, but I suppose it's a first step."

"Hmph. He always talked about how he missed his parents. I don't know what else they taught him, but he's going to have to unlearn at least one of their lessons," Dale mused.

He told her about Brent, how he wasn't getting better physically, but could beat Dr. Barsky and friends he'd brought to their house to play chess.

"So, there's another chance for him, too, I guess," Dale said. "He'll be an expert in chess, and people will come to him."

He also told her about his new opportunities at coaching and writing. But soon they had caught up. Dale found the books he wanted and fished his library card out of his coat pocket. "Uh ... well, I guess I have to go."

"All right." Charlene clucked her tongue. "Goodbye." She went back to the books she'd been reading.

He had almost reached the circulation desk when he reversed, walked back to the aisle, and leaned against the edge of the bookshelf. "I'm coming back next Saturday to get new books for Brent," he said.

He kept his eyes fixed on Charlene, hoping no other patrons were close enough to hear. She kept her eyes on her book.

"We could talk again if you come, too."

She didn't respond. He straightened himself, picked his books up, and began to walk away.

"Dale," Charlene whispered.

He froze, then turned around. Still not looking up, she pulled a book off the shelf, opened it, and scanned her eyes over the pages. "I ... I'll be here. I do my homework at the library." She looked over at the table where her snickering sisters poked each other and stole glances at the two teenagers. "I can leave them at home sometimes," Charlene said. Then she raised her eyes and smiled.

His heart beat fast as the librarian opened the back covers of his books and stamped the date due slips. He tucked the books confidently under his arm and skipped his way up the steps.

AFTERWORD

Polio is a crippling disease that destroys the motor neurons in muscles responsible for movement, swallowing, and breathing. The virus spreads when contaminated feces enter the mouth because of poor hand hygiene. It multiplies in the throat and stomach, and moves through the blood into the central nervous system, damaging the ability of nerves to function. The damage may be temporary, partial, or complete. Every polio patient had a unique experience. To this day, there is no cure, but polio is 100% preventable through vaccination.

While polio has always plagued humanity, epidemics emerged as society developed cleaner habits, children were less exposed to minute amounts of the virus that built immunity, and mothers nursing their babies for shorter lengths of time weren't transferring enough antibodies. Thousands died, mostly children. Hundreds of thousands were paralyzed between 1900 and the late 1950s.

The virus usually swept through in summer months, when children were out of school and playing together. But where it would hit and how many lives would be devastated couldn't be predicted. Terrified parents kept their children away from others, from playgrounds, swimming pools, and theaters. Streets normally teeming with the noise of children's play and bluster fell silent. Among other outbreaks in the United States, two stand out—the first centered in New York in 1916, when 27,000 people were infected and 6000 people, mostly children under five died, and the wave of 1952, which saw 57,000 cases and claimed more than 3000 lives. Between 1949 and 1955, more than 11,000 people in Canada were paralyzed. The worst year in Canada was 1953, with 9,000 people paralyzed and 500 dead. Manitoba was the hardest-hit province, with nearly 3,000 cases and 89 deaths. That year, the virus also attacked adults aged twenty to forty years in large numbers.

There are three types of polio, the first targeting muscles, the second and third affecting the ability to swallow and breathe. Some children found themselves trapped inside iron lungs, fighting for each breath. Until 1928, when the iron lung was perfected, people whose breathing systems were paralyzed by polio most often died.

Entire hospitals devoted to caring for polio victims were built, but the race was on to find a solution—a vaccine to prevent children from getting sick. Through the 1920s and '30s, scientific research was spurred by a campaign started by U.S. President Franklin Delano Roosevelt, who contracted polio as an adult. He started The March of Dimes—an initiative to get people to contribute even the smallest amount of money, to fund rehabilitation for polio victims and research about the disease. All over North America, fundraising activities such as Mothers' Marches and Schmockey Night (where local celebrities played hockey) became recognized events, while children contributed pennies, nickels, and dimes from lemonade and bake sales, car washes and other activities.

The world celebrated on April 12, 1955, when it was announced that trials of a vaccine created from inactive virus, developed by Dr. Jonas Salk and his colleagues from the University of Pittsburgh, had succeeded in preventing children from getting polio. People cheered, church bells pealed, sirens blew, and newspaper headlines proclaimed "IT WORKS!" in big, bold letters. Many, many people admitted they wept openly. Parents breathed a collective sigh of relief; the vaccination promised a safe, healthy future for their children.

This was before Medicare in Canada, when families had to pay for doctors' visits or hospital stays. But the Canadian government stepped up and paid for the vaccines to protect public health. Children aged five to eight years were vaccinated first, then lines of school children waiting for the life-saving injection snaked through gyms. In gratitude to Jonas Salk and his team of researchers, people signed telegrams—such as the one sent from Winnipeg—that stretched 71 yards (65 meters) long.

Then, on April 26, 1955, disaster struck. Eleven children in the U.S. developed polio and died after being inoculated with vaccine formulated by Cutter Laboratories in California. All vaccination programs in the U.S. and Canada immediately stopped, with an investigation launched to discover whether the vaccine wasn't viable, or if it was only the batch at the Cutter Laboratory.

In Canada, the Minister of Health, Paul Martin, had had polio himself, as did his son, Paul Martin Jr. (who later became Canada's 21st Prime Minister). The pressure to cancel the Canadian program grew, but Martin investigated the methods used by Connaught Laboratories in Toronto, where all the Canadian vaccines were manufactured. He satisfied himself that the supply was safe, and on May 7, 1955, declared Canada would continue to vaccinate children as the dangerous "polio summer" approached. Later, he described it as the most important decision he made as a politician.

Martin was right. The rates of polio infection among Canadian children plummeted. An investigation found that Cutter Laboratories allowed a contaminated batch to be shipped. The hot summer claimed more victims in the U.S., before measures were taken to secure the quality of their supply.

A few years later, a liquid vaccine was developed by Dr. Alfred Sabin. Often squeezed onto sugar cubes, it replaced the Salk vaccine, because it was easy to administer. However, because the Sabin vaccine came from live virus, rare cases of polio occurred. In Canada and the United States, the Salk vaccine is now used exclusively.

With the success of vaccines, polio and its dangers

were soon forgotten. But polio victims suffered its effects for the rest of their lives. Those most seriously impacted remained dependent on iron lungs, using frog breathing techniques for periods of time, but ultimately needing machine assistance to survive. Some developed post-polio syndrome in later adulthood. The new nerves the body built were not as strong as the original nerves, resulting in muscle weakness, breathing problems, and other debilitating issues, which sometimes led to premature death.

Dedicated efforts to vaccinate children have now eliminated this crippling, deadly disease on all continents except Asia. From 350,000 cases a year in the 1980s to about 50 in each of the last few years, the goal to eradicate polio is reachable. Polio vaccines are an invaluable tool; they prevent unnecessary misery, save lives, and give children a chance for the healthy, happy lives their parents dream for them, and which they naturally deserve.

A teacher's guide to Second Chances *can be found on the Red Deer Press website.*

TO LEARN MORE

If you want to find out more about the polio epidemic, about Rooster Town and the Métis community, or about NHL hockey in 1955, here are some useful resources.

Polio Sources
Books:
Finger, Anne, *Elegy for a Disease—A Personal and Cultural History of Polio*. New York: St Martin's Press, 2006.

Kehret, Peg, *My Year with Polio*. Morton Grove, Illinois: Albert Whitman, 1996.

London, Joan, *The Golden Age: A Novel*. New York: Grove Press, 2013.

Kluger, Jeffrey, *Splendid Solution—Jonas Salk and the Conquest of Polio*. New York: G.P. Putnam's Sons, 2004.

Offit, Paul A;, MD, *The Cutter Incident—How America's First Polio Vaccine Led to a Growing Vaccine Crisis*. New Haven: Yale, 2005.

Wilson, Daniel J., *Living with Polio—The Epidemic and Its Survivors*. Chicago: University of Chicago Press, 2005.

On-line:
Cherney, Bruce, Great Polio Epidemic of 1953. Winnipeg: WinnipegRealtors, June 12, 19, 26, 2019.

Remembering Polio—The Epidemics of the 1950s. CBC Ideas. Canadian Broadcasting Corporation, 2007.

Métis Sources
Campbell, Maria, *Half Breed*. Toronto: McClelland and Stewart, 2019.

Peters, Evelyn, Stock, Matthew and Werner, Adrian. *Rooster Town—The History of an Urban Métis Community, 1901-1961*. Winnipeg: University of Manitoba Press, 2018.

Schnerch, Marie. *Eddy Street*. Self-published, 2011.

Hockey Sources—On-line:
1955 NHL Stanley Cup Final: DET vs. MTL. https://www.
hockey-reference.com/playoffs/1955-detroit-red-wings-
vs-montreal-canadiens-stanley-cup-final.html

1955 Stanley Cup Final Highlights Detroit vs Montreal.
YouTube.com

ACKNOWLEDGMENTS

Everything that happened to the characters in this story happened to a polio survivor I interviewed or whose memoir I read. I owe a debt of gratitude to the people who shared their personal stories. They recalled the painful events that changed their lives, so children today can learn about the damage infectious diseases can cause, and understand the value of science and vaccines to society. My thanks to them.

Dale Leitch survived polio during the worst epidemic in 1953, but his two-and-a-half-year-old brother, Brent, did not. Their mother, Grace, was also stricken. Although she returned home, she was paralyzed, and needed the assistance of an iron lung until she died in 1980.

In 1952, Paul Alexander was six years old, when he was hospitalized with polio in Dallas, Texas. He assured his mother he would be home in a few days. It would be eighteen months before he did go home, all that time spent in an iron lung, surrounded by a steam tent, with a tracheotomy in his neck, and a ventilator pumping oxygen into his lungs. He has needed an iron lung ever since, but Paul never let the disease define him. He excelled in academics and became a practicing lawyer. For many decades, he was able to leave the iron lung for lengths of time each day, using air gulping techniques. He has also published his own memoir, *Three Minutes for a Dog.*

When the late Charlene Craig developed polio symptoms in August 1951, her mother rushed her by boat from their home in Burns Lake B.C., then flew her from Kitimat to Vancouver. Several hospitals refused them entrance because they were afraid of the virus. When she was able to leave hospital, Charlene remembered the boys serenaded her to the tune of "My Best Girl" by Walter Donaldson, to wish her well.

George Goosen told me the local doctor in rural Manitoba didn't believe he was sick; it was his parents who saved his life by rushing him to hospital in Winnipeg.

Diane Lemon didn't receive a vaccination because her father didn't believe in them, and she fell ill with polio in 1957. When her parents came to visit her in hospital in Regina, they brought Bridge Mixture, a chocolate treat in those days she still remembers fondly. Her father helped her to do her exercises when she returned home, and, influenced by the treatment that helped her recover, Diane pursued a career in the then new field of physiotherapy, rising to become an administrator of medical services. She also volunteered in the sport of synchronized swimming for many decades.

Morley Lertzman was a young medical student when the biggest polio epidemic broke out in 1953. He alternated days working in the emergency department and on the hospital wards. Dr. Lertzman contracted polio himself and was treated at home, but his experience informed his work as a physician until he retired.

This project came to mind after a chat with Mindy Barsky, whose father, Dr. Percy Barsky, developed polio when he was 21 years old. His experience as a patient motivated him to become a pediatrician and help others. Many Winnipeg families recall the attention and kindness he gave children from the 1950s until his death in 1989.

Dr. Peter Salk is the son of Dr. Jonas Salk, who led the development of the polio vaccine. An infectious disease specialist himself, Dr. Peter Salk worked with his father, researching the biology and immunotherapy of cancer and autoimmune diseases, and strategies for vaccine production. He also researched treatments for HIV/AIDS, and currently serves as the President of the Jonas Salk Legacy Foundation. Peter was kind enough to speak with me from San Diego, about being a child in the midst of his father's very public work, and about the difference the vaccine has made to societies all over the world.

Cheryl Currie is the president of the Manitoba Post Polio Network, and put me in contact with many of the people I interviewed. Karen Naylor, Philip Rodgers, and Richard Rice also told me their stories about having polio as children.

The Riverview Heritage Museum in Winnipeg holds the history of the King George Hospital, where polio patients were treated. The iron lung and other equipment collected there added to my understanding of the physical and psychological challenges patients faced, and the difficulty of treating this disease. The write-ups about the caring staff showed how their long hours and dedication were valued.

Many years ago, I met a woman who walked with hand crutches and whose legs were braced. She had suffered starvation during the Nazi occupation of The Netherlands in World War II. Her bones were weakened, leaving her unable to walk without support. Yet she defied expectations, becoming a nurse, immigrating to Canada, and living independently. I only remember her first name—Katie—but I never forgot her example.

Gwen Stewart was a teacher and then principal at Seven Oaks School for three decades. Originally from England, her feisty but caring heart is remembered in her eponymous character.

My uncle, Albert Zaidman (1920–1960), lived with multiple handicaps. To honor his memory, I have him accomplish in these pages what he could not do in life.

Brielle Beaudin-Reimer of the Louis Riel Institute gave me direction and a list of resources, so I could understand the prejudice and exclusion endured by the Métis in Manitoba, and the situation of the residents of Rooster Town. Frank Sais was a teenager in 1960, when the City of Winnipeg expropriated the home his parents, Charles and Elise (Arcand), owned on Hector Avenue, without informing them. They were paid a paltry sum in return, and were the last family to leave Rooster Town. Frank and his son Darrell generously trusted me with the story about how the loss of their home and community impacted their family. Val Vint gave me added understanding of the Métis reality.

My library card got a good workout at Winnipeg Public Library, which has a substantial collection of materials about polio, memoirs of polio survivors, and the history of the Métis in Manitoba. A special nod to the friendly staff at the West Kildonan branch, situated right across the street from the house where Vince Leah lived. Leah, who had polio when he was eight years old, was a fixture in the sports community in Winnipeg for sixty years, joining *The Winnipeg Tribune* in 1930 as a reporter, and rising to the position of sports editor. Leah is credited with giving the Winnipeg Blue Bombers Football Club its name. As well as other supportive activities, he coached youth hockey and soccer. A community center and an area street are named in his honor.

Getting details right about a historical period adds credibility to a novel. Don Kuryk, President of the Manitoba Hockey Hall of Fame and Museum, provided me with oodles of information about hockey leagues, and the community center system in the 1950s. The Museum displays uniforms and equipment used by players at the time, when games were outdoors and spectators froze their toes as they cheered on their friends. Sarah Ramsden, Senior Archivist for the City of Winnipeg, patiently combed through the minutes of City Council and Transit Commission meetings from 1955 to give me an accurate picture of the bus routes, as the city expanded down Grant Avenue. Darrell Liebrecht of SaskTel Pioneers helped determine the telephone utility rates at the time.

My husband, Cecil Rosner, a lifelong chess player, taught my young character Brent the right moves to win a speed game and become a board game phenom. His opinions and the feedback from my first readers— Kirsten Morris (who co-authored the teacher's guide), Beryl Young, Jim Anderson, Karen Burkett, Charlotte Duggan, my aunt Shirley Zaidman, my daughter, Michelle Rosner—made a big difference. My writing group, Voices in Bloom—Laurel Karry, Kathy Tatsu, Kathy Moore, and Tracy James-Hockin were encouraging boosters.

My thanks to Red Deer Press editor Peter Carver, who saw the value in telling these stories to young people. His insight made revising the manuscript an exciting process, and the story is stronger for it. Thanks to Penny Hozy for her keen-eyed copy editing and to the team at Red Deer who contributed to its publication.

The last word belongs to the polio survivors. Each of them volunteered a comment as they summed up their experiences. Two stand out for me: George Goosen said, "Jonas Salk is my hero." Dale Leitch said, "Jonas Salk saved us from further tragedy."

They could do nothing to alter what happened to them, but hoped telling their stories would guarantee a safe and healthy future for others.

INTERVIEW WITH HARRIET ZAIDMAN

What made you want to tell the story of the 1955 polio epidemic in Winnipeg?

I'm interested in how events affect people, and children were the most affected by polio epidemics. I wanted to write about how this terrible virus changed children's hopes and dreams, and how science saved future generations from fear, disability, and death.

Vaccines for polio and other deadly diseases have been so successful that people have forgotten the devastation of the diseases themselves. The anti-science, anti-vax movement that puts children's lives at risk has always troubled me. Proponents of these ideas deliberately spread misinformation and conspiracy theories, which confuse parents concerned about protecting their children. Peddling misinformation is a giant money-making business, even while those who do it condemn profit-making pharmaceutical companies.

Their spokespersons command high fees for lectures, and sell bogus cures that are ineffective against deadly diseases.

The fear and suspicion they generated had tragic results. In 2019, 207,000 people died from measles internationally, mostly children under five years of age, 50% more than 2016—deaths attributed to vaccine avoidance, according to the World Health Organization. Anti-vax advocates accept no responsibility.

Science isn't perfect—sometimes there are mistakes or wrong conclusions. Personalities and politics can cause science to be misused. But we continually learn and improve. Scientific advances take time and investment by governments, who are responsible for our wellbeing—as the program to eradicate smallpox proved. Smallpox killed about 300 million people in the 20th century, until concentrated vaccine programs made it the first disease to be eradicated from the world in 1980. Polio vaccine efforts likewise proved beneficial. For anyone who thinks Covid-19 vaccines are optional, or conspiracies, the stories of smallpox and polio victims are evidence.

John Bryant, a recovering polio patient, reads to children in iron lungs. (Archives of Winnipeg)

The description of the polio ward in the hospital includes graphic details: living in an iron lung, going through rehabilitation with Mrs. Stewart, and the reality that some polio patients did not recover. Why was it important for you to include those details in the story?

I want readers to know the terrifying, debilitating, deadly reality of polio. Anyone who had it wished they hadn't. It's the same for other highly communicable diseases for which vaccines have been developed—scarlet fever, whooping cough, rubella, measles, mumps, and others.

Readers should understand the consequences, and challenge anyone who pretends these illnesses aren't life-altering.

What barriers did polio survivors face after their release from hospital?
It's interesting that while patients were in the hospital, their needs were looked after and they could engage in many activities. As soon as the virus left their bodies, their muscles needed retraining, but they weren't ill. To keep their minds busy and grow as people, they formed musical or drama clubs, wrote newsletters, played games, etc., even some who were in iron lungs.

But what happened after their release was a different story. Polio survivors needing assistance—whether braces, wheelchairs, or iron lungs—faced physical and economic barriers as they tried to move forward in life. While some succeeded, stories abound about constant challenges—from sidewalk curbs to stairs to outright discrimination, leaving many of them socially isolated. This was before laws required wheelchair access and equal opportunity in housing and employment. Some children weren't accepted in school; administrators

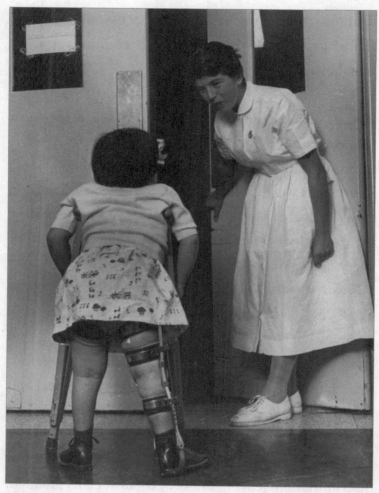

Many children needed braces and crutches to recover their mobility. (University of Manitoba - Winnipeg Tribune Collection)

rationalized a wheelchair-bound child couldn't escape a fire, or other students would be "uncomfortable" around handicapped classmates. Employers rejected wheelchair applicants for no other reason than their disability. The cost of attendants and other assistance stretched budgets to the limits.

Their circumstances as adults coincided with a demand for civil rights in the U.S. during the 1960s and 70s, spreading to other countries. With other "shut-ins," the movement grew, resulting in changes to building codes and housing and employment practices, so the physically challenged can lead productive, fulfilling lives.

Interestingly, some survivors, who'd never considered higher education, continued studying, since they couldn't perform physical work. Some were the first in their families to graduate from universities and become professionals.

Although what's called the post-polio syndrome opened another chapter in their lives, the experience and activism of polio survivors helped pull down physical barriers and influenced society to become more inclusive.

Growing up in Winnipeg, as you did, how much did you know about Rooster Town and its residents?

I only learned about Rooster Town in 2016, through an article in the *Winnipeg Free Press*. Its history reflects how the Métis were robbed of their rights as a founding people of the province of Manitoba, then shunted to the sidelines, literally, based on their race.

Rooster Town began in 1900, a working-class community with mostly Métis residents. About 250 people lived there in the 1930s and '40s, many related by family. The houses, self-built constructions, were spaced unevenly, rather than lined in rows. They had no electricity, running water, or sewers. Outhouses sat behind each property. There were no paved roads, only footpaths.

Why did people live there when, a short distance away, houses had modern amenities? Because the Métis were discriminated against. They were descended from European fur traders who married Indigenous women. When Canadian settlers moved west, the Métis resisted the takeover of their land. Ultimately, their resistance, led by Louis Riel, was defeated in 1885.

They were promised "scrip" or land entitlement, but the promises weren't honored. Unlike First Nations,

The Laramee family, residents of Rooster Town, Winnipeg. (Courtesy of the Laramee Family)

who were assigned reserves after they were displaced from their lands, the Métis were dispossessed. They weren't accepted into the settler society, either, because they were partly Indigenous. Their "half breed" status meant they were a people in between, which led to injustice and impoverishment.

In some areas, the Métis had difficulties buying land or renting homes, forcing them to live along edges of highways on road allowances, without any services. "Rooster Towns," "Dog Towns," or other similar communities developed on the prairies. In Winnipeg, the

Métis built homes on land the city hadn't developed. It's thought the name came from residents owning chickens or because they "roosted" on the land. Those who owned properties paid taxes, but received nothing in return.

Many Rooster Town residents worked for the railway companies, for the City of Winnipeg, in landscaping, construction, or other working-class jobs, often because they didn't have the money for higher education and better paying jobs.

Discrimination started early. Former residents said their mothers sent them to school scrubbed clean—not just because they were good parents, but also to disprove a lie to children from nearby streets. Some parents told their sons and daughters that the Rooster Town children were dirty because of where they lived, and because they had dark skin. Some recall their fellow students wouldn't hold hands during a game or dance. Articles about Rooster Town in the newspapers were contemptuous, never failing to mock the poverty of the residents, rather than investigating why people lived as they did.

The Canadian economy boomed after World War II. Returning soldiers married and began families—the

Houses in Rooster Town, Winnipeg. (Archives of Manitoba)

"Baby Boom" generation. Developers wanted land to satisfy the demand for new houses. With the cooperation of the City of Winnipeg, they campaigned to expel the residents of Rooster Town, offering each household $75 at first, then lowering the amount to $50, to relocate. Although residents resisted, they had no political allies or lawyers to press their case. The Sais family was the last to leave in 1960. The homes were bulldozed or burned, their presence erased by new houses, linked to electricity, water, and sewage, and lined up on smooth, organized roads. The Métis families dispersed, many to the working-class North End of Winnipeg.

In this era of reconciliation, Canadian society finally acknowledges the racist treatment of Indigenous, Inuit, and Métis peoples and the harm done to them and subsequent generations. The losses Rooster Town residents experienced—their homes, their family structures, their culture, are now recognized.

Why was it important to you to include Charlene in this story?

I asked Dr. Morley Lertzman, who worked at the King George Hospital, if certain populations were harder hit than others. He said, "Everyone got polio." So, I read newspapers from that time, and realized that was when developers had their eyes on Rooster Town. I included Charlene to inform today's young readers about this shameful episode.

More and more, Indigenous, Inuit, and Métis writers are telling their stories. By including a character from Rooster Town, I hope to help make young readers think about how damaging racism is, and how wrong it is to allow racism to influence decisions about relationships.

You've chosen to tell Dale's story in third person, rather than first person. Why did you make that decision?

I imagined myself as Dale, what he thought and how he felt. When Dale played with Brent in the yard or argued with his father, I imagined it was me. I did that with all my characters, actually. But when I wrote, I stood back so I could "see" or have more perspective, which I used as the story progressed.

One important aspect of Dale's story is his relationship with his father. Why is it that we see Dale needing to educate his father about the dangers of polio, rather than the other way around?

We rely on our parents to teach us about life. We usually believe them, then support and propagate their views. But sometimes parents are stuck with old ideas, stereotypes, superstitions, or prejudices they can't shake, either from "loyalty" to their own parents, or because it's hard to admit you're wrong.

Dale chooses to question Dad's illogical beliefs, even though they clash. He loves Dad, but wants facts to guide them, not conspiracies (several months after his claim about white coffins was broadcast, Walter Winchell admitted it was fabricated) or illogical conclusions (that Dad's grandfather should have lived because his family paid for the operation, or that because Dad recovered from scarlet fever, no one else should suffer the life-altering complications of congestive heart failure, kidney damage, or hepatitis).

For Dale, getting Brent vaccinated was crucial. He appeals to Dad's intelligence, to give him a second chance to study information about the vaccine.

It's the same for Lindsay, who accepted and continued his parents' racist attitudes. He learns the hard way that they're not acceptable, hopefully giving him a second chance to realize healthy relationships should be based on someone's personal qualities, not their race.

What aspects of the polio epidemic would be useful for readers to consider as we deal with the Covid 19 pandemic and its aftermath?

We should act on history's lessons and do better. The polio epidemic (and others before) taught us we should take positive measures to protect public health and build unity in society. When governments invested in scientific research and committed to universal vaccinations, the polio epidemic ended.

We're used to asserting our personal rights. But we also have responsibilities to others. We follow speed limits, stop at red lights, and wear seat belts because those rules prevent car accidents and death. They aren't conspiracies to take away the right to drive freely.

The Covid-19 pandemic tragically demonstrated the need to teach the lessons of history and reinforce what social responsibility means. Denying facts, attacking science and public health orders were destructive— in the cost of human lives, the monetary cost, and the divisions in society.

I wrote this novel before the pandemic, but as Covid-19 unfolded, it was disheartening to see that in the 21st century, some people still promote irrational medieval superstitions. When the Black Plague swept Europe in 1349, it was declared that Jews were putting the bacteria into wells where people drew water. In the ensuing hysteria, two thousand Jews were burned to death in Strasbourg, France, and thousands more murdered in other cities.

Yet the plague continued, the bacteria carried by fleas.

Manitoba's Mass Thank You telegram to Dr. Jonas Salk was sent over CNR telegraph wires. It carried more than 8000 signatures, was 200 feet in length, and took eight hours to send. (University of Manitoba - Winnipeg Tribune Collection)

Racists and rightwing politicians linked themselves with anti-vax ideas during Covid-19, using inflammatory language to blame China for the virus—and by extension anyone of Chinese origin, no matter where or who they were. They raised anti-Semitic tropes and other racist stereotypes, leading to physical assaults and death threats that echoed ignorant, dark times of the past. They protested that governments and scientists were taking away "freedoms" through public health orders to wear masks or limit gatherings. Some religious communities claimed their right to worship was being denied, but had no explanation for why other religious groups supported public health measures and vaccines to protect society—and their lives.

Yet, the virus didn't care. It mutated and killed even more people.

The results were catastrophic in countries where chaos ruled. At least six hundred thousand people died in the United States, supposedly the most scientifically advanced nation. The health systems in Brazil and India collapsed. The contrast with countries that followed rigorous protocols to prevent illness and death is shocking.

You are obviously interested in the history of your hometown of Winnipeg, considering your previous novel, *City on Strike*, and this one. What is your message to young readers interested in exploring the histories of their own communities? Why is that exploration so rewarding?

My message is that there are universal, meaningful

stories right in front of you, no matter the community. The important stories are about how ordinary people's lives are changed by events and decisions.

When you interview people who lived through different periods in history, you'll find "ordinary" people are quite extraordinary. Our society is built through their fortitude, resilience, and principles.

I'm glad I interviewed my parents about their childhood, for example. Their stories of family, school, and the neighborhood added richness to daily life in *City on Strike*. I'm glad I heard firsthand from polio survivors for *Second Chances*. I appreciate that people recorded their memories of these events.

It's rewarding to translate research into stories that make readers feel like they were there. People of different ages—an eleven-year-old, a sixteen-year-old, a 75-year-old, told me my writing made them feel they were part of the crowd on Bloody Saturday, June 16, 1919, fleeing the batons of the Mounties and Specials in Winnipeg. They told me they identified with Nellie and Jack's anguish as if it were theirs. They told me they learned how people were treated and how the strike's defeat affected society. They also told me they recognized the parallels between the situation then and society today.

Learning from history—the reason I write.

Thank you, Harriet, for the care you've taken with this story, and for your insights.